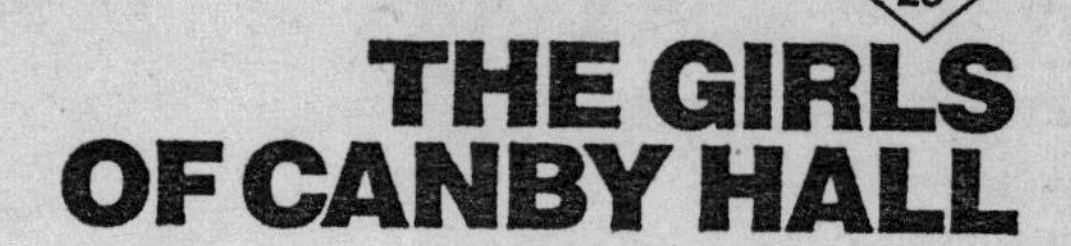

BUT SHE'S SO CUTE

EMILY CHASE

SCHOLASTIC INC.
New York Toronto Lonaon Auckland Sydney

Scholastic Books are available at special discounts for quantity purchases for use as premiums, promotional items, retail sales through specialty market outlets, etc. For details contact: Special Sales Manager, Scholastic Inc., 730 Broadway, New York, NY 10003.

ISBN 0-590-40833-X

12 11 10 9 8 7 6 5 4 3 2 1 7 8 9/8 0 1 2/9

Printed in the U.S.A. 01

First Scholastic printing, August 1987

23

THE GIRLS OF CANBY HALL

BUT SHE'S SO CUTE

23

THE GIRLS OF CANBY HALL

Roommates
Our Roommate Is Missing
You're No Friend of Mine
Keeping Secrets
Summer Blues
Best Friends Forever
Four Is a Crowd
The Big Crush
Boy Trouble
Make Me a Star
With Friends Like That
Who's the New Girl?
Here Come the Boys
What's a Girl To Do?
To Tell the Truth
Three of a Kind
Graduation Day
Making Friends
One Boy Too Many
Something Old, Something New
Friends Times Three
Party Time!
Troublemaker
The Almost Summer Carnival
But She's So Cute

CHAPTER ONE

The large, brown package that petite Andrea Cord had wrapped in her slender arms was almost bigger than she was. She struggled under the weight of the box loaded with unknown goodies from home, wondering what her parents could have sent her this week that was so heavy and bulky. It felt like enough supplies to keep her two roommates and herself in snacks for the rest of the year. But Andrea knew better than that. In the next week or so, another "care" package would arrive.

Andrea smiled as she thought of her loving family back in Chicago. Leaving them had been one of the hardest things she'd ever done. She thought of her brothers, Ted and Charlie, and her baby sister, Nancy, the one who seemed to change the most each time she saw her, and she felt a stab of homesickness. But Andrea had to remind herself that coming to

Canby Hall had been something she wanted more than anything. Even though she got lonely sometimes, she wouldn't want to go back to Chicago and go to school. Canby Hall had become her life now and she loved it.

Coming around the corner at almost that exact moment was another small girl who was equally burdened with bags and baskets as she rushed to finish the tedious job of moving into her room at Baker House. Only a few days before, a terrific storm had nearly flooded out the basement of Canby Hall and knocked several windows out with the high winds and driving rains. Charles House was harder hit than Baker, and some of the girls were forced to move from leaky, unsafe rooms until they could be repaired. With so little time left in the school year, the board had decided to relocate the girls and undertake the necessary repairs over the summer.

Looking something like two locomotives on a collision course, the girls crashed into one another. Both screamed as packages flew in all directions. Andy's heavy box burst open, and the contents spewed out across the floor. The other girl's suitcase popped open on impact and spilled clothes into a heap near her feet. Both girls said, "I'm sorry," nearly in unison.

Andy got to her feet and held a hand out to the girl who was still sitting on the floor with a dazed expression on her face. Andy wasn't sure if it was because of the fall or the fact that

Andy was one of the few black girls at Canby Hall. As it turned out, it was neither.

"I've never seen so much food," the girl drawled in a soft Southern accent as she stared at all the packages of cookies and tins of crackers and cheese spread around her.

"My family owns a restaurant and they think I'm starving to death up here."

"Must be nice," she said reaching longingly toward a foil wrapped package of chocolate chip cookies that had burst open.

"Help yourself," Andy said.

"Thanks." The girl took one of the golden cookies from the tin foil in her hand.

"Oh, by the way, I'm Andrea Cord, but everyone calls me Andy."

"Oh," the girl said as if remembering her manners all at once. She wiped her hands on the leg of her slacks and extended it to Andy. "I'm Penelope Vanderark." An infectious smile spread across her face. "Isn't that just the craziest name? Actually, it's a family name." She took another bite of her cookie. "Hmmmmm. These are great."

"Have another one," Andy offered.

Reaching into the package she pulled out another cookie. "I suppose Penelope was all right for my mother and my grandmother," she said getting back to the subject of her name. "They're both very dignified and . . . well . . . *Penelope-like*. My family isn't like most families when it comes to nicknames, but with me, daddy made an exception and I've been Penny almost since the day I was born." She finished her cookie and her story almost simultaneously.

When the two of them stood up, Andy was surprised to find she was actually taller than Penny. At only 5′1″, it was unusual for Andy to find many girls she was taller than. Looking at Penny's delicate build, Andy was surprised Penny had knocked her down. When they had collided, Andy had been sure she'd been run over by an All-American linebacker.

Penny leaned forward to pick up a package of cheese, and her long brown hair fell forward, framing her face in soft curls which set off her large dark eyes. Her eyes reminded Andy of Bambi's, while her cute nose tilted slightly upward completed the pixie image she had.

While Andy was scrutinizing Penny, Penny was busy sizing up the beautiful black girl standing next to her. She had noticed her in English, but Andy was always with two other girls, so they'd never really talked before. Penny'd noticed the great looking clothes Andrea always seemed to be wearing. Today was no exception. She had on a cotton sweater of soft pink and turquoise with pink sweat-pants and matching turquoise socks that folded down neatly over her Reeboks.

Andy picked up the foil package and offered Penny another cookie. Penny said, "Are you sure?" and almost licked her lips at the idea of another homemade chocolate chip cookie.

"Take two. There's plenty."

Breaking into a wide, sunny smile that lit up her whole face, Penny said, "Thanks," and lifted two more cookies from the foil. "Here. Let me help you get this cleaned up," Penny said. She put one cookie delicately in her mouth and cradled the other carefully in the palm of her hand while bending down to help Andy collect the spilled food.

"I really am sorry," Penny said again with her mouth full of cookie. "I guess my daddy's right. I'm a regular accident looking for a place to happen." She giggled musically and Andy found herself smiling at this bubbly new resident of Baker House.

"Daddy said he really hoped I could survive being sent away by myself without anyone to look after me, but so far, everyone's been real helpful. Thing is," Penny said looking around, "daddy should have been worrying about the other guy." She laughed again sending tinkling sounds echoing down the hallway.

Andy went across the hall to reach the last package of popcorn. "Want me to help you take these to your room?" Penny asked.

"Sure, if you want to. But it's right here," Andy said, nodding toward 407. Penny was only able to carry a package of crackers and a small container of cheese while Andy managed to get the rest of the things back into the broken box and juggle it in the direction of her room.

Andy set the box on the floor next to her bed while Penny looked at the room she had just entered. It certainly showed an odd combination of decorating. Her mother would have a fit if she saw this room. Looking at one corner in particular, Penny noted that the absence of maids at Canby Hall was quite obvious.

But still, the room did have a certain charm. It was a comfortable room. One bed, covered in a modern print of earth tones, must have been Andy's. At least she had set the box beside it. The desk by that bed was neatly organized and above it hung posters of ballet dancers.

Another bed had a rainbow comforter, but little other decoration. As Penny followed the line of the wall up to the ceiling, however, she saw what she was sure was a tea bag hanging above the bed. Surely, it had to be some sort of potpourri.

The last corner held a bed that appeared to have a cross-stitch quilt on it that matched the blue in the walls, but there were so many things on the bed, that the spread only peeked through in a few places. The desk top, chair, and bedposts were all buried beneath mountains of clothes and books and empty soda cans.

"Come on," Andy said, "I'll help you with your things now." Penny led the way out into the hall. Her things were still lying in a clutter.

Penny began shoving things into a suitcase and forced the lid down. Even with sitting on the suitcase, the latch refused to catch. Penny looked at Andy almost apologetically and shrugged. "I never was much of a packer."

Struggling with the suitcase which she was trying to carry down the hall without spilling, Penny led the way to her room. Andy had picked up the wicker basket that must have doubled as a garbage can and began collecting an assortment of plastic bottles of lotions, books, shampoo, and odds and ends. She could see the suitcase sticking out on either side of Penny's slim figure, with clothes trailing from it at comic angles. Andy decided it was a lucky thing Penny couldn't get the thing closed, because she'd have never been able to open it again.

Andy followed Penny into a room that was so cluttered, it made Jane's area look neat and organized. Boxes in different stages of unpacking were setting all around the floor. Clothes were hanging from boxes and the foot of the bed and stacked on the chair. Penny noticed Andy's expression and said, "I'm not much of an *un*packer either."

Pushing some of the boxes aside, Andy worked her way toward the dresser. She began taking things out of the basket and setting them on the dresser top in a neat row. "Oh, never mind about that," Penny said flopping onto the bed which was covered with a layer of clothes, but no bedding, "I'll do it later."

Penny raised her hands high above her head. "I sure wish Mom was here. I hate stuff like this and she's so good at it. Actually, she's good at telling the maid what to do." She sighed dramatically. "I suppose that's something I'll have to learn if I'm ever going to be able to run my husband's house one day."

"Well, it'll be your house too," Andy said.

"Oh, of course it will."

"Who is this lucky guy you're in training for?"

"I haven't found him yet, silly. Once I start college then I can really begin looking."

Andy looked at Penny with disbelief and moved over next to the bed. She lifted a pile of clothes from the seat of the chair and set them on the floor so she could sit down. She took a wrinkled pillow case from the bed and smoothed it out before she folded it. "Why don't I help you with this? I don't have anything to do until dinner."

"Gosh, are you sure?" Penny said sitting up.

"I'm sure. I love organizing things."

Another giggle answered Andy's remark. "You sound like my mother," Penny said. She reached for a sweatshirt and began to fold it. "When I enrolled at the beginning of the semester, Mom and our maid Diane helped me get settled. Then that big storm blew the top off everything, and suddenly we had as much water falling through the ceiling as there was pouring outside the window."

Andy watched the haphazard manner in which Penny was folding the sweatshirt. Her own towel had been carefully folded so all corners lined up perfectly. She set it at her feet and reached for another one.

"Well, daddy was just horrified that I was living in this leaky room, and I had to tell him that that was no ordinary storm. It took all my persuasive talents to talk him into letting me finish out the year. My roommate, Jessica, went on home until next fall. Course, I didn't know then that I was going to have to move myself into this new room. But I guess it was either this or a houseboat." She laughed.

The whole time she was talking she kept trying to fold the sweatshirt in her lap, but something always seemed to go wrong with it. The arms would fall out or the top would unfold. Finally she sort of rolled it into a ball and tossed it to one side. Andy had by then neatly folded at least six things while Penny had mangled the one.

"I think daddy called Ms. Allardyce and asked to have me moved. It sounds like something he'd do." She laid back on her bed again and didn't notice Andy reach for the sweatshirt Penny'd just folded so she could redo it. "He thinks I can't do anything for myself."

Looking at the mess around her, Andy thought Penny's father might have a good point there.

"Tell you what," Andy said. "Why don't I fold these things and hand them to you and you can put them away?" Penny got to her feet and took the things Andy handed her. She opened one drawer then another and finally set them on top of the dresser. "I'll organize this stuff later when I have time to plan it out."

Penny told Andy most of her life story while Andy cleared the things from the bed, thinking wryly to herself that at least Penny would be able to sleep in her bed tonight. Provided, that is, that she could make a bed!

Penny had been raised in the family's historic house outside of Atlanta, Georgia. She was the youngest of three children, but her two older brothers were in their teens when she was born. And she missed all the love and attention she got at home, even though she did like Canby Hall.

Listening to Penny talk, Andy thought that Penny made her roommate Jane Barrett seem self-sufficient. And up until now Andy had always thought Jane, with her proper Boston upbringing, was one of the messiest girls at Canby Hall. It looked like she was about to have some competition.

Andy heard voices in the hall and glanced down at her watch. It was five-thirty. She was supposed to be meeting her roommates, Toby and Jane, in Room 407. She set the last sweater on the bed and said, "I've got to be going. I told my roommates I'd meet them at five-thirty. They've been at the library working on that English paper we have due the week after next."

"Oh," Penny said, the bright light fading from her eyes. "Thanks for all your help." Andy turned toward the door. She opened it and looked back. Penny stood in the midst of the chaos like a rejected child. Andy had the feeling Penny might not have anything more than chocolate chip cookies for dinner if she didn't ask her to come along.

"If you don't have any other plans, you can come along with us," Andy offered.

Penny's face lifted. "Gee, that would be great. I hate eating alone and since my roommate left yesterday, I've been pretty much existing on junk food from the vending machines downstairs."

"I'll meet you in my room in ten minutes," Andy said on her way out.

Chapter Two

Andrea came into Room 407 to find her two roommates, Jane and Toby, examining the box she'd received from home. Jane's long blonde hair tumbled into her face obscuring her view of the door, and she didn't see Andy enter. Toby looked over and saw Andy standing in the doorway. She cleared her throat loudly.

"Just a minute," Jane said impatiently. "It looks like there's a whole bunch of goodies in the bottom I haven't even searched yet."

Toby cleared her throat more loudly and gave Jane a slight nudge before saying, "Hi, Andy."

"Andy?" Jane said standing up abruptly. "Andy," she said, smiling at her with traces of guilt all over her face. "I didn't hear you come in. We were just . . . uh . . ."

Actually, Andy didn't mind at all that her roommates were looking through the box of food her parents had sent her. They always sent enough to feed an army. But she did enjoy seeing Jane's proper Boston manner in a state of flutter. Jane always appeared so all together and unaffected. She was from the "Barretts of Boston," one of the oldest families in Massachusetts. In fact, her family had come over on the *Mayflower*. When Jane invited them to her family's annual "Barrett Landing Party" a few weeks back, Andy had joked that her ancestors had arrived in a big ship too. They'd just been riding below deck.

Jane hadn't thought it was nearly as funny as Toby and Andy did, but then they'd discovered Jane took her family's ancestry very seriously and it was no joking matter to her.

Andy was enjoying the momentary discomfort of her proper roommate who had been caught with her hand in the cookie jar, so to speak. But enough was enough. She didn't want her best friends thinking that they weren't welcome to anything she got from home.

"Never mind," Andy said, smiling at her. "You guys know that anything I get from home is fair game. We're roommates, right?"

"Right," Toby said with enthusiasm.

"Oh, right," Jane said with relief. "I just didn't want you to think that we'd be snooping around and take anything without asking."

"It's okay," Andy said again. "You don't

have to ask. You know you're welcome to anything I have."

"Well, just the same," Jane said straightening up, "I think you should know that one of those packages of cookies is already open. In fact, the whole box looked like it arrived air mail without a parachute."

"Yeah," Toby said. "Like dropped from five thousand feet."

"Well, I had a little accident in the hall on my way in. The box broke open, and one of the packages of cookies spilled out."

"What a shame," Jane said shaking her head with remorse. "It was chocolate chip, wasn't it?" Andy nodded. "They're my favorite kind."

"Penny's too."

"Who's Penny?" her roommates asked in unison.

"Penny is the accident I had in the hall. Well, actually, we both ran into each other, and I guess it was as catastrophic for her as it was for me."

Toby said, "I don't remember anyone named Penny living in Baker House."

"She's just moving in. She was in Charles House before the big rains came. Her roof sprang a giant leak, and they moved her over here."

"You say her name is Penny?" Jane said moving toward her side of the room and tripping over a pair of rolled up sweat pants on the floor. She stumbled and made an uncharacteristically sloppy landing on the edge of her bed. "I don't believe I know her," she said trying to regain her dignity in spite of the clumsy fall.

"You ought to," Andy laughed. "The two of you keep house just alike. Besides, I think you'd recognize her if you saw her. I've seen her around myself a few times, but I didn't know her name."

"Well, maybe we'll stop in after dinner," Toby said getting up from Andy's bed. "I'm starving and I want to get over to the cafeteria and eat dinner so I can come back here and load up on dessert." Her eyes went back to the broken box on the floor near Andy's desk.

Toby was from a small town in Texas called Rio Verde. The other girls had their suspicions that she'd eaten one too many meals on the trail. She was one of the few girls at Canby Hall to actually *eat* the school's food. Most of the girls would pass it up or choke down small amounts to fight off malnutrition, but Toby actually *liked* what they served.

Her mother had died years ago, and she was raised by her father and the hired hands on their ranch in Texas. When she first came to Canby Hall, she was more at home in the wilderness than the city. It had been a difficult adjustment for her, but she was learning what her father had hoped she'd learn: how to get along with other people.

But that was as far as the lesson went. In

spite of his hopes for her, Toby's dream was to finish school and go back to Texas and run the ranch. She loved horses and land and no amount of schooling would ever change that.

"Let's get going," Toby said impatiently.

"You don't have to wait to meet her," Andy said. "She's having dinner with us."

"Okay. Where is she? I'm starving." Toby started toward the door.

"She'll be here any minute. You'll like her, Toby. She's from the South. Just like you."

Toby felt herself bristle at the implication that she and this Penny person might be anything alike. She had a pretty good idea what this girl might be like. One of those southern belle types.

"Let me get one thing straight right now," Toby said firmly. "Texas may be in the South, but we don't grow southern belles out there like they have in some southern states. Just because we both say 'y'all' every now and then, doesn't necessarily mean that we're going to have a lot in common."

"Just don't jump to any conclusions until you meet her," Andy reasoned. "I really think you two will hit it off."

They didn't have to wait long to find out if Andy's predictions were true. Almost on cue, Penny timidly knocked at the door. Toby, who was nearest to it, pulled the door open. Penny peeked in and smiled at everyone.

Andy came over to her. "Hi, Penny, come

on in. Guys, this is Penny. Penny, meet my roommates, Jane and Toby." She pointed to each girl and they both nodded and said, "Hi." She was struck by the odd contrast in the three roommates. Andy with her dark skin and hair stood next to Jane with her long blonde curls and blue eyes. And nearest her was Toby with her red hair and green eyes. They would have had to work hard to have found three girls that looked more different.

While Penny analyzed her three new acquaintances, Toby was busy sizing up Penny. She certainly looked the southern belle type; helpless, sweet. In fact, Toby felt herself flinch when Penny opened her mouth and spoke with a soft voice, steeped in southern warmth. She looked over at Andy and shook her head. How could Andy have ever thought the two of them would have anything in common?

"I can't tell y'all how nice it is of you to let me come along. I just hate eating all by myself," Penny said shyly.

"Well, you can eat with us anytime," Andy offered.

"Sure," Jane agreed. "That is if you can eat that slop they serve over there."

The four girls went out of the room, Toby bringing up the rear and watching Penny. Jane and Andy seemed totally taken in by this new girl, but Toby had seen girls like Penny before. She'd have to explain all about them to Andy and Jane later on.

On the way to the cafeteria, Penny started telling the girls what a chaotic first couple of weeks she'd had at Canby Hall. Transferring in mid-year hadn't been easy. Everyone else already knew their way around campus and she kept getting lost. Toby had a feeling this girl would have gotten lost if she'd arrived on the first day and been given a guide dog to lead her around.

Jane and Andy were flanking her on either side, thoroughly enjoying her amusing story about how she'd met Patrice Allardyce, the school's headmistress, for the second time.

"I stopped a senior girl and asked her where the library was. She pointed out Ms. Allardyce's house and said, 'Just walk on in. It looks like a house, but that's the whole idea. You're supposed to be comfortable in there.'

"Well, I thought it was a great idea. I opened the door and saw this large room with paneled walls and lots of books, and sitting right there on the table was this tray with tea and cookies. I couldn't believe it. Real southern hospitality right on the East Coast. I sat right down to have a snack before I started searching for the card catalogue, and this lady comes up behind me and says, 'May I ask what you think you are doing, young lady?' "

Penny's imitation of Patrice Allardyce, better known to the girls as P.A., when she wasn't around to hear it, really had them laughing. Even Toby found herself cracking a smile.

"But that wasn't the worst part," Penny continued. "When I turned around and saw who it was, I was so surprised to find out that she was the librarian as well, I choked and spit cookies and tea all over the beautiful wooden coffee table and the plate of cookies she had set out. From the look on her face, I knew I'd been had, and I realized I'd walked right into her house and made myself at home."

"Oh, my gosh," Jane gasped between giggles, "What'd you do?"

"At first she just stared at me like she thought I was a bad dream. Then I started to cry, that always works with my family," Penny confided. "Then I told her the whole story. Before it was over, she got us more tea and cookies and we ended up having an awfully nice time."

"That makes you something of a celebrity around here," Andy said. "Not many of us have had tea and cookies with P.A."

They went into the cafeteria and got in line. Each girl took a tray and moved along selecting things she would be willing to take a chance on eating.

"The one thing I find interesting about this place," Penny said, "is their resourcefulness. For instance, have you noticed that they have one kind of Jell-O for dinner, so they put it under a slab of wilted lettuce on this end and that will be our salad. Then they drop a blob of white stuff on it down at the other end and that's tonight's dessert."

"How long did you say you'd been here?" Jane asked. "It sounds to me like you have our Canby Hall cafeteria figured out pretty well."

"Actually, I think it's a plot to keep us from getting fat," Andy said. Seeing Maggie and Dee, the girls that had the room next to theirs, Andy said, "Let's sit over there."

Andy introduced everyone, and it looked like everybody at the table was interested in Penny's life story except Toby. Toby watched Penny's animated face hold them all spellbound while she told about getting lost in a shopping mall when she was a baby.

"I was just about the friendliest little thing that ever was," my mama said. "And she started to pay for this swimming suit and when she turned around, I was gone. Of course, I always had a thing for mirrors. I used to love to make faces in them." She made a face by scrunching up her nose and crossing her eyes. Everyone laughed and Toby decided she probably *still* made faces at herself every morning. "So they checked all the dressing rooms first.

"When they still hadn't found me twenty minutes later, they blocked off all the entrances and made an announcement about this missing baby. My mother was in a panic with all the missing kids you read about all the time. She was trying to figure out what she was going to tell my dad. She was always losing things, her purse, her car keys, now she'd have to call him and explain how she'd lost the baby. She just didn't think he'd understand at all.

"Just as she was going to call my daddy and tell him what had happened, a lady came up the aisle carrying me in her arms. She asked if this was the missing baby and said she'd noticed these packages of men's underwear flying into the air across the aisle from her, and when she went around the bin to look, there I was sitting inside this little cubicle throwing underwear all over the floor."

All the girls laughed at Penny's crazy story and then launched into their own stories about having been lost when they were little kids. None of the stories seemed to have the same humor as Penny's. She had a way of telling things that made you laugh with her. Jane had a feeling if she were to try to tell it to someone else, it wouldn't be nearly as funny.

After dinner, Penny left the girls at the top of the stairs and went in the opposite direction to her room. "I've got to try and shovel through all that stuff before Monday or I may never find anything until the end of the year."

"Good luck," Andy said. "If you need any help, I'll be around in the morning. Just come on down."

"Yes," Jane agreed. "Come down anytime."

She smiled at Toby and Andy. "It can be lonely without roommates."

At first, Jane had wanted just that, a room to herself, and she was angry and antisocial when she discovered she'd been given, not one, but *two* roommates. But now, she wouldn't trade room assignments with anyone at Canby Hall. The three of them were like a family.

They got into the room and shut the door. "Isn't she a riot?" Andy asked.

"Oh, yeah," Toby said, flopping onto her bed and staring at the tea bag on the ceiling above her bed.

"What's the matter, Toby?" Andy asked. "You were awfully quiet at dinner."

"How was I supposed to get a word in edgewise?"

"Come on, Toby," Jane said, "She was probably nervous, and she wanted to make a good impression. I thought she was funny."

"I thought she was an airhead!"

"Hey, Toby, give her a chance," Andy said. "You don't even know her yet."

"Yeah, but I know the type. They can't do anything for themselves. I met my share of them back in Texas, and I don't think there's anything funny about them." She turned her back to her roommates, and both Andy and Jane knew it was best to leave it alone for the night. Toby would come around.

CHAPTER THREE

While Toby lay on her bed lost in thought about what it was that she found unsettling about Penny, there was a knock at the door. Andy answered it.

Meredith Pembroke, the housemother of Baker, was standing in the hallway outside Room 407. As usual, she was dressed casually in slacks and an oversized blouse. Her dark hair was pulled loosely back. She looked almost like a Canby Hall student herself.

Of course, in a way, so had Alison, the previous housemother, who always had looked like she'd just stepped out of the Sixties. After Alison left in mid-year to get married, it had been a real adjustment to get used to Meredith.

And it wasn't just the way she dressed — at first — that was different from the way Alison had done things. In the beginning she practically had every girl at Canby Hall on the verge of expulsion with her nonstop demerits. But things had settled down some since the beginning. The girls had found out that Meredith was pretty human and had made a few mistakes herself when she was younger. In fact, she had been one of the wildest girls in school. After the secret was out, thanks mostly to Meredith herself, things fell into place at Baker, and the girls started to like their new housemother.

Andy stepped back and opened the door wider. "Come on in," she offered. Meredith nodded politely and entered the room.

Jane stood up and scowled at the clothes lying at her feet. "I was just going to clean up this mess." The chaos Jane had on her side of the room had gotten all three of them demerits when Meredith first arrived.

"That's good," Meredith said, her eyes twinkling and a smile playing on her lips. "But that's not why I'm here. Ms. Allardyce is holding a special meeting at 10:00 tomorrow morning about the open house this month and she asked that the three of you be there."

"Sure," Jane said. It must be something important if P.A. was holding the meeting personally. "You can count on us."

"Good," she let herself break into a real smile. "Since it's only 8:15, Jane, that'll give you plenty of time for your weekend cleaning."

She turned to leave the room. Meredith closed the door on her way out. Andy sat down at her desk. "I still miss Alison," she sighed.

Toby sat up and for the first time took an interest in the conversation. She looked at the two of them. "What do you think she wants?"

"Probably has some important job for us," Jane said.

Toby looked at Jane. "But why us? We're only sophomores. You'd think if it was really important, she'd give it to the seniors."

"Well, you never know," Jane said. She got up and started picking up the clothes scattered on the floor around her bed. She got the laundry basket from the closet and began bunching things up and tossing them in. If she was going to be tied up all day tomorrow, she'd better start on this tonight, she thought. Before Meredith came, she had been contented to let it go for weeks at a time.

At 9:00 the next morning, Andy's clock radio clicked on and began filling the room with sound. Jane rolled over and crammed the pillow onto her head.

Andy got up and came over to her, pulling the pillow off her face. Groaning, Jane looked up through one sleepy eye. "It can't be morning already."

"It is and as long as it takes you to come around, you'd better get up now or you'll be late for that meeting with P.A." Jane rolled back on her side and pulled the covers up above her head. "Don't expect Toby and me to wait for you if you're not ready," Andy warned, as she padded out into the hall to the showers.

Andy didn't bother to check on Toby. She was already up and gone. She'd probably had breakfast and been out to Randy's to ride this morning. Randy was a guy whose family owned a ranch just past the school's boundaries. Toby had met him the first week of school and they'd been good friends ever since. Toby enjoyed being able to ride at Randy's, but Andy had a suspicion that it was his brotherly advice and concern that she liked the most. Each of the roommates had found ways to combat bouts of homesickness. The ranch was Toby's.

Andy came back into the room to find Jane pulling herself slowly to her feet and Toby already dressed for the meeting. At least Andy assumed she was probably going like she was.

It had taken the girls a while to get used to Toby's laid back style of dressing. She felt at home in jeans, sweatshirts, and boots, and she looked good in them. And, with Jane and Andy's help, she knew now how to look just as good when she'd dressed up for some special occasion.

Andy selected a pair of Hawaiian print shorts in red, teal, and lavender and pulled on a matching T-shirt of bright red. She combed her soft black hair and dabbed at the tips of her long lashes with mascara. Most of the girls at Canby Hall wore very little makeup.

Jane came back from the shower wrapped in a soft pink terrycloth robe. She had her hair wrapped in a white towel and she reminded Andy of a stuffed Easter Bunny. Andy smiled. "What's so funny?" Jane asked.

"Nothing," Andy said hastily. Jane didn't have the best sense of humor in the mornings.

When they got to the library, where they were to meet with Patrice Allardyce, the girls found an assortment of sophomores, juniors, and seniors. Sitting down, they asked the girls next to them if they had any idea what the meeting was about. No one seemed to know.

Patrice Allardyce appeared shortly to end the suspense. She was wearing a tailored grey suit, her blonde hair pulled back in its usual twist, looking somewhat like a New England version of royalty.

"Girls, if I may have your attention." The room quieted down quickly. Ms. Allardyce didn't have to ask twice. "I suppose you're wondering why you had to get up on a Saturday morning and meet with me." She smiled at them before setting her glasses on the podium.

"As you know, we're having the open house at the end of this month. The purpose of this open house is to let interested girls have a first-hand look at Canby Hall and find out how we operate here.

"A very important part of all of this, is you, the girls. We like our visitors to see how exhilarating life at Canby Hall can be. We know the reason most of their parents are considering Canby Hall is for our excellent academics. And while we know how important that is, we can't overlook the friendships that are formed here that last a lifetime."

Ms. Allardyce took a minute to look around the room. Jane felt her eyes stopping on the three of them and she sat up a little straighter. Andy felt the warmth of friendship she shared with her roommates. Toby, getting bored, just wanted the headmistress to get on with what she was going to say so she could go out and enjoy this beautiful spring day.

"All of the girls here play an important part in the annual open house. Some of them will work with the decorations and the clean up of the campus. Some will help plan the banquet. But I have a special job for each of you. I want you to serve as guides for the prospective new students.

"I have carefully chosen those of you that I feel have formed a special bond that exemplifies the best of Canby Hall. I am hoping those friendships will serve to show the new girls what they can expect to find at our school."

She picked up a list of names from the

podium. "Now in just a few minutes, I'll be giving you names and addresses of the girls for whom you'll be responsible. But first, I want to give you an idea of what I hope you will do for them.

"I'd hope you'll begin by writing them a letter telling them about yourself and how anxious you are to meet them. Now, Saturday is already planned out for you. We'll have a tour of the school and a nice luncheon with an opportunity for the girls to meet the housemothers, instructors, and myself. And then that afternoon, there will be a variety of things to attend, from cultural to sporting events.

"I am hoping you will plan to do something Saturday night that will be typical of a weekend at Canby Hall and enjoyable for you and our guests. This doesn't have to be anything elaborate. Just some simple activity that shows the girls what a nice place we have here." She smiled warmly at them.

"Remember, girls, this is your chance to put your best foot forward for Canby Hall. I'm counting on you." She held the list up and said, "Now, as I call your names, please come forward and get the names and addresses of your girls. They've been assigned by rooms, so one girl can come forward."

While P.A. began the tedious task of calling off names, Andy, Toby, and Jane began brainstorming on things they might do on Saturday night.

"Maybe Cary will be playing that night and we can all go see him," Jane suggested hopefully. Cary played with a band called Ambulance. In fact, that was how he and Jane met. She had gone to a dance to research a paper she was writing for a creative writing class, and he had been playing.

Jane had never been able to explain the attraction they had for each other. They seemed to be on opposite sides of just about every issue there was, but some magnetic force seemed to pull them constantly toward each other.

"Yeah, or we could go on a hay ride at Randy's," Toby suggested. Jane wrinkled her nose at the thought of lying in a stack of itchy, prickly straw while being pulled through the woods by horses.

"But that's not typical of what we do here on Saturday nights," Andy said. "You guys are missing the point. P.A. wants us to show them what they can expect to do on the weekends if they come to Canby Hall."

"How about nothing," the girl next to Jane said. She was a junior from Charles House. "That's what we usually do." Ms. Allardyce called her name and she went up to the podium.

"Why don't we write the girls and find out what they like to do?" Jane suggested.

"That's a great idea," Andy said.

Toby shook her head. "I think it's asking for trouble."

"Why?" Jane and Andy asked.

"Because they probably like to do some ridiculous thing that we don't have around here."

"Then what do you suggest?" Jane said. "And don't say horseback riding."

"I wasn't going to. I think we ought to come up with a couple suggestions and then write the girls and tell them what they are and let them decide from there."

Andy put her arm around Toby's shoulders. "Sometimes we don't give you enough credit." She smiled at her. "That's a great idea."

Toby smiled back. "Naturally. I'm a great kid."

CHAPTER FOUR

Andy wiped the moisture from her brow with the yellow terry cloth sweat band she had around her wrist. She faced the mirror and continued the strenuous stretching and conditioning exercises she did routinely as a part of her dance warm-up.

The music broke into a rock beat and she backed away from the bar and began to improvise a jazz dance. She leaped and turned and moved her lithe body rhythmically to the beat of the music. She loved being alone in the studio and letting herself go crazy. Just allowing the music to fill her up and take her where it wanted her to go. She imagined herself dancing for Baryshnikov like she'd seen him dance in the deserted theater in one of her favorite movies, *White Nights*.

Andy was so absorbed by the music and the mood, she didn't hear Penny come into the studio. Penny stood back and watched the flowing movements and the total abandonment with which Andy danced. She was spellbound. She had no idea her new friend was so talented.

The music ended and Andy, breathing deeply, collapsed onto a bench. She heard the applause and she looked sharply toward the door in surprise. Penny noticed the look on Andy's face. "I'm sorry, I stopped by the room, and Jane said you were probably over here. I hope you don't mind my barging in."

"No, of course not," Andy said. She reached for a towel and dried off her face and neck. She leaned back against the cool cement wall behind her and shut her eyes briefly. Actually, she did mind a little. This was a magical time when she let herself be anything she wanted, and she didn't like someone intruding on her fantasy. But the moment was already lost and there was no use making Penny feel bad about it now.

"Did you get everything unpacked?" Andy asked as she pulled herself up from the bench and began to stuff her things into her dance bag.

"Well, kind of," Penny admitted. "Jane stopped by earlier this afternoon after you guys got back from the meeting and she sort of helped me out."

Andy smiled to herself. That ought to be like the blind leading the blind, she thought. She looped the shoulder strap of her dance bag over her shoulder. With her other hand she reached down and picked up the radio she'd been playing. Andy started outside and Penny fell into step beside her.

"I hope I didn't cut your practice short," Penny said, a worried scowl wrinkling up her face.

"No. I was about wrung out for this afternoon anyway." They stepped out into the late afternoon sun. A gentle breeze was blowing through the tall trees around them and fanned Andy's yellow dance leotard.

"You know I used to think there wasn't any place on this earth more beautiful than the South with all the magnolia trees and the ivy covering everything, but looking around here on a day like today, I have to admit, I may have been wrong."

Andy looked around her. Trees were breaking out in new growth and lush green leaves hung above them like a rich green canopy. The flower beds were popping out in all sorts of spring colors.

Andy felt a rush of love and belonging. This was all hers to enjoy. She felt lucky to be a part of it. She thought about the new girls that would be arriving for open house in a few weeks and knew they would fall instantly in love with the school.

"I didn't know you were such a terrific dancer," Penny said, quickly changing the subject. "How long have you been at it?"

"I've probably been dancing since I could walk. But I only decided I wanted to be a professional dancer a few years ago."

"A professional? Isn't that scary? I mean, think about it. Hundreds, no, maybe *thousands* of people are out there practicing every day to make it and you're one of them. If it was me, I'd just give up."

"No, you wouldn't," Andy said. "Not if it's your dream. You wouldn't care if there were a million people out there."

"Come on, Andy. I don't have your determination or talent."

"You must care about something. What is it you want to do with your life?"

"What do you mean?"

"Well, surely, there's something you want to do one day."

"Sure there is," Penny said with a contented smile. "Get married."

"Is that all? I mean, there's more than that that you want for yourself, isn't there?"

"Like what?"

"Like a career, for instance?"

Penny giggled and threw her head back, tossing her long curls back and forth behind her. "I can't do anything special," she said.

"Of course, you can. Everyone has special talents. You just haven't discovered yours yet. Why, I bet that's why your parents sent you to Canby Hall."

"My daddy sent me to Canby Hall because

he wanted to be sure that I would be prepared for a good Ivy League college."

"See?" Andy said.

"So I could meet the right husband," Penny said authoritatively.

"But what about you? What about your goals?"

"Those are my goals. To get married to some wonderful man who will take care of me just like my daddy does. And I'll be a wonderful wife to him, just like my mother is. And we'll have wonderful children and a maid and we'll all be real happy."

"That sounds like a Mother Goose fairy tale."

"Well, what's wrong with that?" Penny asked.

"I'll tell you what's wrong with it," Andy said, feeling her frustration mounting. "You have to have dreams."

"That is my dream."

"That's your parents' dream. What's *your* dream?" Andy asked, feeling exasperated at Penny's acceptance of the cut-and-dried future her parents had carved out for her.

"I don't know what you want me to say!" Penny said smiling uncertainly and looking almost ready to cry. "I'm not like you, Andy. It might be different if I could dance or sing or act or something, but I can't. I hate the sight of blood, so med school is out. I'm afraid or heights, so that kills any hopes of me being an astronaut."

A smile crept across Penny's face and lit up her eyes. "Besides, what's wrong with letting someone else take care of you? Why should I go off to work every day when I can live with someone who will do it for me while I play golf and tennis and go to the movies with my friends?" They turned up the walk toward Baker House.

Andy shook her head and smiled back at Penny. She was the kind of person you couldn't stay mad at for very long. And she was also the kind of girl that some successful guy was going to love taking care of.

At the top of the stairs, Andy turned toward her room. "I got to get a shower before dinner. I'll stop by later tonight and see how the room arranging is coming."

"That'll be good," Penny said. "There's still a couple of things I need to take care of."

Andy went into her own room. She set the radio on the desk and dipped her shoulder, allowing her dance bag to slip easily off and drop to the floor. Jane looked up from her desk where she was working on some great masterpiece, no doubt. Jane wanted to be a writer one day, and she worked hard at it. Andy looked at Jane who, like Penny, had led a pampered life. Yet she had set goals for herself.

"Did Penny find you?"

"Yeah," Andy said, sinking down onto the chair to rest for a minute before she took her shower. "What are you doing?"

"I'm working on an article to submit to the *Canby Hall Journal* next week."

"What journal?" Toby asked coming into the room. She looked as if she'd been out riding horses. Her short red hair was a mass of tangled curls and her cheeks were flushed from the warm spring afternoon.

"Ms. McArthur told our creative writing class all about it. Each spring they publish a journal that's a collection of short stories, essays and poetry. All the material is written by Canby Hall students. A lot of future writers have written for that journal. But, the important thing is to be able to tell agents and editors someday that you've had work published," Jane said.

"Agents and editors? What are you writing?" Andy asked, getting up and coming over to the desk to peer over Jane's shoulder.

Jane pulled her paper closely to her chest. "It's not ready yet. When I get finished I'll show it to you."

Andy backed away. "Then I'll go take a shower while you complete your masterpiece." She grabbed her soap and her towel and went out into the hall.

Andy stepped into the rushing water and felt the warmth of the spray surround her. Her thoughts went back to the conversation she'd had earlier with Penny.

How could it be that anyone wouldn't have a desire to do something special with her life? She couldn't imagine her own life without her dreams. What would be the point? Penny had to have some special talent that she just hadn't discovered yet. It was up to Andy to help her find it.

Chapter Five

Andy came in from her last class Thursday, exhausted and happy that it was nearly the weekend. She went to their mailbox and pulled the letters from it. As usual, she had a letter from home. It seemed between all her family, she got something almost daily that was fun. Poor Toby hardly ever got mail.

Andy readjusted her books on her hip and began thumbing through the few letters in their box. She found a letter addressed to Toby. The handwriting wasn't her father's and she knew by the postmark that the letter was from April Wilson, one of the two girls they would be hosting.

She ran up the stairs to the room and burst through the door. No one else was there. Andy knew that Jane was at the library working on her entry for the journal. She saw the clothes Toby had worn to class were folded and lying on the foot of her bed and guessed that she'd probably come back and changed so she could go riding at Randy's. She might not get back until dinner, and Andy wanted to know what was in the letter now.

She held it to the light and tried reading it through the envelope. She shook it around inside and found no matter what she did, she couldn't tell what it said. She tested the corners of the flap to see how securely it was sealed, but there was no give and she was sure to rip it if she tried to pry it open.

"I have a letter opener," Penny said from behind her. Andy jumped. Penny laughed. "What are you trying to break into anyway?"

"Toby got this letter from one of the girls who'll be coming to open house, and I was anxious to see what it said. She hardly ever gets mail, and I don't think I ought to open it without her consent."

"Where is she?"

"Out riding at Randy's, I think. She probably won't be back for at least a couple hours." Andy tossed the letter on the desk and plopped into the chair beside it.

"Well, how far is it to Randy's? Why don't we take the letter to her?"

"That's a great idea," Andy said. She got up and went to the dresser and pulled a pair of jeans out. "Let me get changed and we'll go find her."

"I'll meet you in my room when you're ready," Penny said. Andy pulled on her jeans and hung her skirt in the closet. She put her shoes back in their box and got her tennis shoes down. She kept all her shoes in boxes and labeled each one. Jane and Toby laughed at her, but she never had to climb around in the closet on her hands and knees ducking under clothes to find the mate to her other shoe like Jane often did.

She went down to Penny's room. The door was slightly ajar. When she knocked, it swung open. Andy surveyed the chaos.

The boxes were pretty much where they'd been before. Some of them appeared to be unpacked now. There were sheets on the bed, but they were all bunched up at the bottom. The clothes Penny had been wearing earlier that afternoon were lying on top of a pile of things that appeared to be the other clothes she'd worn this week. The bottles were still lined up on the dresser where Andy had left them last week. She was surprised anyone could live in such a mess — except maybe Jane.

Penny appeared not to notice the look of dismay on Andy's face. "Come on in, I'm almost ready." Penny was slipping into a red nylon jogging suit. She bunched her bright yellow socks around her ankles and slipped her small feet into white hightops.

"You might want to wear some other shoes," Andy said. "Those look pretty new. It's liable to be muddy crossing the orchard to Randy's place."

"These will be okay. If they get muddy, I'll send them home to my mom," Penny said smiling.

"Do you wear the same size shoe?"

"No, she'll clean them up for me before I get home."

"Are you kidding?" Andy asked in disbelief.

"Yes," Penny giggled. "I'd *never* send a pair of muddy tennis shoes through the mail. I'd just stuff them in the closet or shove them under the bed until I could take them home." She turned and got a yellow ribbon from the top of the dresser and tied it around her long dark hair drawing it into a ponytail at the back of her head.

"Well, I'm all ready."

They went out into the late afternoon and felt the warmth of the sun. It was pleasant, but not hot yet. The mugginess of summer hadn't set in.

They walked past the main building where most of the classes were held and behind the library. There was a small orchard that was in full bloom. The pink blossoms filled the spring afternoon with their scent.

"Just imagine all the apple pies and turnovers and cakes you could make out of these when they're ready," Andy sighed, thinking about the homemade desserts her mother featured daily in their restaurant.

"Maybe you could make them, but I'm sort of a disaster in the kitchen. After I accidentally substituted salt for the sugar in some hot chocolate I made one time, my mother said the only way she'd let me back in the kitchen was if I took home ec.

"That sounded like lots of fun and so I signed up for it in the eighth grade. Just before Thanksgiving, we made cinnamon rolls. We had home ec the last period of the day and our job was to clean up the kitchen units and put the rolls in the freezer for a breakfast we were having for the faculty the Monday after the holiday.

"Well, we wrapped all the rolls in foil and put them away and wiped down the kitchen area and went home. When I got to school early Monday morning for the breakfast, Mrs. Johnson, the home ec teacher, met me at the door with a scowl on her face. She told me that I'd forgotten to take out the last pan of cinnamon rolls from the oven before we left."

"You're kidding?" Andy said.

"The cleaning crew found it after the pan had been in the oven for three hours and they were *done*." Penny said with a smile and a shrug of her shoulders. Penny and Andy both laughed at her story and the sounds of their merriment bounced off the trees around them and filled the orchard.

"You're lucky you didn't burn the school down."

"That's what Mrs. Johnson said. We moved on to a sewing unit, but I didn't do much better there. I accidentally hemmed my dress to the skirt I was taking up, and she had me transfer to creative writing."

They came out on the other side of the orchard and saw stables and a big white house. One of the horses was contentedly nibbling on a bundle of hay near the barn. Andy looked around but didn't see Toby.

"She might be out riding," Andy said. "Let's just sit down and wait for her to get back." They sat at the base of one of the big apple trees.

Andy leaned her head back and closed her eyes. No wonder Toby loved it out here. It was so restful. The sounds of birds singing around her lulled her into a peaceful state of near sleep until the sound of hooves pounding on the road startled her and she jumped. She got to her feet and saw Toby and Randy riding up the road. Andy went toward them with Penny walking by her side.

Randy was riding the big palomino, and next to him was Toby on the little filly she'd helped Randy break in last fall. He'd even let her name the horse. She'd decided on Maxine because her horse back in Texas was Max.

"What a great looking horse," Penny said, but from the look on her face, Andrea thought she was more interested in the rider than the horse. Randy made quite a picture in his flannel shirt and jeans. His blond hair was windblown, and his cheeks were already beginning to tan from the early spring sunshine. He looked like a model for a Marlboro billboard, except, of course, he didn't smoke.

"I don't believe we've met." Randy extended a hand toward Penny. "Randy Crowell."

"Randy, that's Penny Vanderark," Toby said with a hint of annoyance in her voice. This was her place, and she didn't like the idea of Penny showing up here and invading her world.

"Guess what," Andy said with excitement. "Look what came for you today." She held out the letter and Toby reached for it. She looked at the postmark and ripped at the envelope impatiently. She pulled out the neatly folded stationery inside.

"Must be something good," Randy said to Penny. "Maybe it's from that guy in Boston," he said with a smile. Jane's old boyfriend Neal, who was actually more of a family friend, had formed a friendship with Toby that seemed as mismatched as that of Jane and her current boyfriend Cary.

"Actually, it's from the girl she'll be hosting during open house," Penny explained.

"No kidding. More recruits for the old institution." Penny looked at him sharply. "Sorry. I'm not real crazy about Canby Hall girls."

"Why not?"

"Long story."

"What about Toby? She's a Canby Hall girl."

"That's different." He looked back over his shoulder. "Toby's special." Randy took hold of the reins of his horse and began leading it toward the stable. Penny tried to decide what kind of relationship Toby and Randy had. He didn't seem upset about the fact that she might be reading a letter from some other guy.

"I really do like your horse," Penny said. She gingerly reached out to touch the flank of the powerful animal.

"Want to take a ride?" Randy asked.

"I'm not sure I could," Penny said, her eyes widening. "I mean, he's so big."

"But he's real gentle." Randy patted his horse affectionately on the side. "Aren't you, boy?"

Toby rode over to them with Andrea following behind. She dismounted and began to lead Maxine into the stable to take her saddle off and brush her down.

"What about that horse?" Penny said as Toby walked past them. "It's a lot smaller."

"*It* is a she and she's also a lot wilder," Toby said.

"Oh."

"You don't have to ride. I just thought you might want to, that's all." Randy began to lead his own horse toward the stable.

"No, I'd love to ride," Penny said quickly. "I just want you to be sure and watch me so I don't do anything dumb. Like fall off." Penny smiled and her eyes seemed to dance flirtatiously from the horse to Randy.

"Okay, I'll hold onto the reins and you get on. That ought to be safe enough." Penny giggled again. Toby pulled the saddle from Maxine. She tossed it over the fence and turned around where she could lean against the fence and watch. This ought to be good, she thought to herself.

Suddenly she stood up straighter. Penny expertly slipped her left foot into the saddle and gripped the mane with her left hand and the saddle horn with her right hand. She made a helpless attempt to pull herself up and then dropped back onto the ground in a heap of hopeless laughter.

"He's just too big," she giggled. "I don't know what I'm doing." Randy came around to help her up, but Toby realized that Penny knew very well what she was doing. It was just a small thing, but an inexperienced rider would have grabbed the saddle horn with her left hand and the back of the saddle with her right. This girl had ridden before.

If Randy had seen what happened, he

ignored it and hoisted Penny's tiny body easily onto the horse. She looped her leg over the saddle. "Now hold on tight," Randy said, "and don't worry about a thing. I'll lead you." He took the reins and began walking the horse in a slow easy circle.

Toby turned away and took hold of Maxine's reins. "Looks to me like that horse isn't the only one getting led around," she said to Maxine. "It's just that the horse knows who's leading him, and Randy hasn't caught on as to who has him by the nose."

Toby went into the stable and got the curry comb and began to brush Maxine down. Outside, she could hear the sounds of Penny's laughter and her squeals of delight as Randy got on behind her and the two of them raced off toward the pasture.

She came out just as they galloped back. Randy had a firm hold on the reins and an even firmer hold on Penny. Toby picked up her jean jacket and slapped the dust from it. "We'd better get back to school or we'll miss dinner," she said curtly.

Penny slid from the horse and landed squarely on the ground. "That was just the most fun, Randy. Someday I'm going to have to come back here and learn how to do it all by myself."

"Anytime," Randy said getting off the horse and stepping down beside her. His cowboy boots made him look even taller and he towered over Penny's tiny five-foot frame. He began walking with her toward the gate.

"Toby comes out quite a bit, I'm sure she wouldn't mind you coming along once in a while." Randy missed the cold stare Toby sent his way. "Just be sure that you don't ever try getting on him without me around. I'd hate to be responsible for any more injured Canby Hall girls." He put his arm around Penny in a protective gesture and winked at Toby.

Randy was referring to an incident earlier that year when Toby had taken off on Maxine in a snow storm and had gotten thrown. She had sprained her ankle and Randy had found her half-frozen in a snow bank. Toby liked to think of herself as independent and it wasn't one of her fondest memories.

"I wouldn't even try it," Penny assured him. No, Toby thought, she probably wouldn't. It wouldn't be near as much fun to ride horses if there wasn't someone around she could put on a show for. And Randy was the perfect audience. He was buying every line she fed him. Sometimes boys were such dopes.

Chapter Six

It was after dinner before the girls got a chance to discuss the letter from April. Between the "riding lesson" for Penny and Jane's losing track of time at the library, they almost missed dinner as it was.

Andy sensed Toby was upset about something, but she wasn't sure what it could be. Andrea knew that Randy and Toby were just good friends, and she didn't think that Toby was jealous of the attention Randy gave Penny. But Toby sure had been acting funny ever since she'd seen Penny and Randy at the ranch.

They came in from dinner and Andy flopped down on her bed. Toby sat on the foot of her bed and pulled the letter from her pocket.

"April sounds like she'll be lots of fun and really nice," Toby said. She opened the letter and read, "I'm sure that anything you want to do Saturday night will be fun. I'm so excited about coming that I'd be happy to sit around the dorm and talk all night. I bet it's like one continuous slumber party. I can hardly wait to meet all of you."

"Well," Jane said, taking the letter and rereading it for herself. "Looks like that puts the ball back in our court."

"Translate that for us non-country club people, huh?" Andy said.

"We followed your great idea, Toby, to write the girls, and from the sounds of it, they're not going to care what we do so we might as well plan something that we'll all enjoy," Jane said.

"I suppose that doesn't include a camp-out at the Crowell Ranch?" Toby teased.

Someone knocked on the door and Jane said, "Come in."

Penny pushed the door open and Toby almost groaned aloud. She wasn't up to another evening of "Anecdotes by Penny."

"I'm going to the library," Toby said getting to her feet. "I've got to work on that project for American History."

"But wait a minute," Andy said. "We still don't know what we're going to do about Saturday night and you need to write April back and let her know something."

"You decide," she said, grabbing books from her desk top.

"Is this for the open house?" Penny asked eagerly.

"Yeah," Andy said. "We're trying to decide what to do Saturday night. So far we don't seem to be able to agree on much of anything."

"Why not just go into Greenleaf, grab a hamburger and see a movie? I'm sure no matter what you do, they'll have fun. I mean, who wouldn't have fun with you guys?"

"That's a great idea," Jane agreed. "It might seem dull to us because we do it all the time, but to them it'll be a new adventure."

"Thanks, Penny," Andy said. Then she turned to Toby and Jane. "It's all settled then? We'll go to Pizza Pete's and then see a movie."

"Gosh, that's so original," Toby said. "Why didn't I think of it?"

"I think you're missing the point," Jane said. "Originality isn't the important thing here."

"Thank you, Ms. Barrett."

"Jane's right," Andy said. "It's our friendship that P.A. wanted us to show them. Let's not end it by arguing about how we're going to go about it."

"You guys are so lucky," Penny said sitting at the foot of Andy's bed. "You're going to have so much fun. I almost wish I'd waited until next fall to enroll instead of coming in in mid-year. Then maybe I'd have gotten to spend a great night on the town being entertained by y'all." She laughed.

"I think you'd be the one doing all the entertaining," Jane said.

Andy's face lit up. "Why don't you come along with us next weekend?"

"Me?" Penny said.

"Sure. Have they assigned you to any special job for the open house yet?"

"Well, no, but. . . ."

"Then come with us and help us entertain the new girls."

Toby felt her blood boil. First Penny giggled her way into Randy's life, and now she was barging in on this, too. Toby had a feeling that if she moved out tonight, Penny would be relocated in Room 407 by bedtime.

"Don't you think you should ask P.A. first?" Toby said. Everyone looked over at her. "After all, she did ask us specifically because we're roommates. She might not like us dragging extra people along."

"You're probably right," Penny said. Toby could almost see her eyes glisten with tears. "It's the three of you she wants them to meet. And besides, she probably has some other job she set aside for me, like showing the girls how to find the library." Everyone laughed uneasily.

"I better get back to my room." Penny got

up from the bed. "I still have a mess of unpacking to take care of. Ask Andy!" She nodded brightly toward Andy who couldn't help but smile. "I'll see you guys in the morning."

Penny shut the door and the silence hung heavy in the room. "Well, guess I'd better get to the library," Toby said, but her heart wasn't in it anymore. Penny was gone and there was no reason to leave. However, from the looks on Jane's and Andy's faces, she thought it might be better for her to clear out and let them cool down.

Toby was at the door before Andy's voice stopped her. "If they have a book on etiquette, check it out, why don't you?"

Toby turned back around and smiled uneasily. "What do you mean by that?"

"You, of all people should know what it's like to feel all alone. I can't believe you would deliberately be so cruel to anyone." Andy was really upset. "What did Penny ever do to you? She's trying really hard."

"Sure she is," Toby scoffed. "Just like she tried hard to learn how to ride that horse this afternoon."

"So that's it. You *are* jealous!"

"Jealous. Not on your life. I'm just not as easily taken in as some people. For your information, your new friend isn't as dumb as she pretends to be. I take that back, she's probably just as dumb, but not nearly as helpless."

"What are you talking about?" Andy demanded.

"Figure it out for yourself. I have better things to do with my time." Toby stormed out, slamming the door behind her. She went down the stairs and outside. The warm spring night was much too lovely, and Toby was much to angry to spend time sitting in a library.

Toby headed on past the library, behind the main building and through the orchard to Randy's. She saw him in the corral feeding the horses. She stopped at the edge of the trees though. What would she say that wouldn't sound like some jealous kid? If Randy was as taken in by Penny as everyone else, she'd be wasting her breath anyway.

What she really wanted was to get on Maxine and ride away — just keep going until she got back to Rio Verde where people might be plain and simple, but you could always count on them being genuine.

Chapter Seven

Outside, Toby sat down and leaned against one of the trees while she tried to think things out. Why was it that she had taken an almost instant dislike to Penny, and it seemed everyone else was crazy about her. Was Toby the only one who could see through the act she put on? If she said anything to anyone now, they would think it was out of jealousy. Why Toby would ever envy anything about someone like Penny was beyond her comprehension.

The sky was turning dark around her. It was getting later and she still had some math to do. She'd have to worry about this some other time. Penny certainly wasn't worth flunking anything over.

Walking back across the darkening campus, Toby relished the peaceful night. She never felt afraid at the idea of being alone, even in the dark. She understood nature, it was people that caused the problems.

She made up her mind that if she couldn't change people's minds about Penny by telling them what she was really like, Toby would have to show them. Or rather, Penny would have to do it. Toby felt almost certain that if she let things go a while, Penny would goof up again, like she'd done with the horse, and someone was bound to see her for the imposter she was.

Toby came into the room to a cool reception from Andy, who looked up briefly from her math book before dropping her head again. Toby looked at Jane's desk, which was now empty. "Where's Jane?" she asked.

"Making a phone call," Andy said.

"Oh." Toby pulled her desk chair out trying not to scuff it noisily across the floor. She sat down and opened her math book. After the open spaces of the orchard, the room felt stifling and confined. She was having trouble concentrating. Toby got up and opened the window slightly. The screech drew Andy's attention again. "Sorry," Toby shrugged. She sat back down.

Jane floated back into the room with a dreamy smile on her face. Toby assumed she had been talking to Cary. "How're things at Oakley Prep?" Toby asked.

"Great," Jane said confirming her hunch. Oakley Prep was the nearby boy's school that Cary attended. Unlike Andy, Jane seemed to have forgotten all about the incident earlier with Penny. The phone call had left her smiling and content.

"They're playing in town tomorrow night. You guys want to come along with me to hear them?" she asked eagerly. Andy finally looked up from her desk.

"Sure," Toby said enthusiastically. It wasn't that she was that crazy about Ambulance, Cary's band, but she was anxious to restore the unity she thought was a little shaky right now.

"I guess so," Andy said.

"Look, why don't we invite Penny too?" Toby heard herself saying. It surprised her almost as much as it shocked Andy and Jane. But Toby realized that if she was going to get the others to see what she saw in Penny, she'd have to spend some time with her.

"It'd be a good way of showing her that we didn't mean to be rude when we said she couldn't come along during open house."

"*We* didn't say it," Andy reminded her. "*You* did."

"Okay," Toby conceded. "So I made a mistake and it was rude, I'm sorry."

"I'm not the one you should apologize to," Andy said.

The idea of apologizing to Penny almost gagged Toby, but she said, "Okay, the next time I see her, I'll apologize."

Andy smiled. "Thanks, Tobe, I know it's not easy for you to do that. But I think we'll all feel better about it."

Toby thought Andy might feel better about it, but she'd just feel like an idiot. Well, it might be the price she'd have to pay to get Penny off guard and allow her to make some dumb mistake.

Toby didn't have to wait long to humble herself. The next morning, the three girls were walking across the campus from the cafeteria and saw Penny coming down the steps of Baker House.

"Aren't you eating?" Andy asked.

"I forgot to set my alarm. There's barely enough time for me to get to class, let alone the cafeteria."

"By the way," Toby began feeling self-conscious about the whole stupid apology idea, "I'm sorry if I sounded rude yesterday."

"Oh, don't worry about it," Penny said with a wave of her hand. "I'm not." Andy beamed and felt contented that all of her friends seemed to be hitting it off at last.

"Guess what," Jane said. "Cary's band is playing in town tonight and we're going to hear them."

"And we want you to come along," Andy said.

"That would be fun," Penny said. "I love dances. I only wish I could dance like you.

But I'm afraid when it comes to dancing, I have two left feet sometimes. I wish I could dance like you do," she said turning to Andy.

"I can't believe you can't dance," Andy said.

"Well, I was in a tap class for two months when I was four years old."

"See?" Andy said.

"What happened? How come you quit?" Jane asked.

"The teacher suggested I pursue something else. It seems I spent more time making faces in the mirror then dancing. While all the other little girls worked on their shuffle-ball-change, I was busy practicing my facial expressions."

"Did you ever go back?" Andy asked.

"Nope. My mother cried a lot, packed up my dance shoes, and enrolled me in an acting class."

"I'm glad to see you got some good out of that," Toby said. Everyone stared at her. "I mean, you found a place to practice all the facial expressions," she added quickly.

They walked toward first period, Penny, Andy, and Jane all talking excitedly about that night. Not one of them noticed that Toby was saying very little. What was it about this girl that she didn't like? *Was* she jealous? Her friendship with Andy and Jane had been rocky and difficult in the beginning, and maybe she resented this intruder waltzing into their lives so easily.

* * *

The band was warming up when they got there. Cary saw Jane and he gave her a welcoming smile. Penny stood on her tiptoes and tried to get a closer look at the band.

"Which one is Cary?" she asked.

"The tall one in front with the white jacket. He's the lead singer," Jane pointed out proudly.

Penny studied the boy standing center stage near the microphone. She was more than a little surprised that this was the boy Jane was so crazy about. He wore a powder blue T-shirt with a white cotton sports jacket and black jeans.

He had a very cute face, but his silky brown hair was too long for her taste. It was the small earring pierced through his left ear that really drew her attention, though.

She wondered what Jane's parents thought of Cary. Why, her daddy would keel over dead if she brought someone like that home. She was sure that her parents would have been shocked to find out that there were boys like him at Oakley Prep. Her father had envisioned a campus of miniature Yale and Princeton preppies all majoring in business finance.

Cary jumped from the stage in one easy leap and came over to them. He put his arm around Jane and welcomed them. "I saved you guys a special table." He pointed to a table near the corner of the stage. "Best seat in the house."

"Cary, this is Penny Vanderark," Jane said. "Penny, this is Cary." Jane gave Cary a dreamy-eyed look, and Penny took a closer look herself at his handsome face. With a haircut and the right clothes, he could be a doll. He sort of reminded her of the guy Rob Lowe played in a movie she'd seen a couple years before.

"Well, the guys are turning up. I've got to get to work." He pecked Jane's cheek lightly and hopped back onto the stage and picked up his guitar. The band began to play and Andy started to move. It was as if the music sent vibrations through her and she was on her feet in an instant. She grabbed a guy named Roger, who was sitting at the table next to theirs. Andy had danced with him quite a bit at the last social. She pulled him onto the floor.

"Is she always that shy?" Penny asked Jane with a laugh.

"She loves to dance and she doesn't always want to wait for someone to ask her."

One of the other boys who had been sitting at the same table as Roger came over and bent down next to Penny. "Want to dance?" Penny smiled warmly.

"Sure. Why not?" She got up and he led the way to the dance floor. They stopped next to

Roger and Andy. In spite of Penny's professed lack of dancing ability, she was a very adequate dancer, Toby noticed. Jane, however, didn't notice anything, except Cary.

Andy and Penny didn't make it back to the table until the first set ended. As soon as a song was over, there was some other guy waiting to dance with them. That wasn't unusual for Andy; her reputation as a great dancer kept her busy all night.

The set ended and while Roger walked Andy back to the table, about five guys escorted Penny. All of them seemed to be fairly tripping over themselves to walk next to her. They looked down at her adoringly and all five of them seemed to be wearing that same goofy grin that Randy had had on his face when he was helping her onto the horse.

"Thank you all for seeing me safely back to the table," she said batting her long lashes. "I believe I'd better rest a minute and get ready for the next set."

The boys stood around awkwardly for a minute, hoping in vain for an empty chair, before they started drifting off with comments like, "Well, save me a dance," and "I'll be back."

"This is just the most fun," Penny enthused. "I'm glad you asked me along."

"You look like you're doing okay out there for someone who doesn't really dance," Toby said, trying to keep the edge off her voice.

"It must be Cary's music." Penny laughed as Cary approached the table. "I'm usually the type that trips over the lines they paint on the gym floor."

"Well, whatever you're doing, keep it up," Cary said smiling at her. "You look great from where I'm at." Toby thought she caught a momentary frown from Jane, but it was gone too quickly for her to be sure.

Two of the boys that had walked Penny back to the table returned a few minutes later. They came from opposite sides of the room and both of them set a Coke in front of Penny at the same time.

"How nice," Penny said. "I was getting terribly thirsty." She smiled up at both of them as they stared at each other with a mixture of surprise and annoyance. She took a dainty sip from each one. The music started again and both boys asked her to dance at once. "I'd love to," she said. She got to her feet. "Come on, Toby. Dance with Lance while I dance with Robby, then we'll trade."

Toby noticed the one who must have been Lance turn sharply at the table and stare at her. She wasn't eager to get fixed up with Penny's cast-offs. "That's okay," Toby said. "I'd rather watch. Ole Lance can wait for you on the sidelines, can't you, Lance?" Toby couldn't resist a wicked little wink at him.

The rest of the night consisted pretty much of watching Penny expertly manipulate the boys from Oakley Prep. She danced and laughed and talked and giggled her way through every dance. Toby believed even if Penny *did* have two left feet, not one guy would have ever noticed. Why was she the only person who could see what Penny was doing?

Chapter Eight

Sitting in English, Toby was trying hard not to fall asleep. The lush, green lawn was inviting her to come out and run barefoot through the grass and lie in the shade of the big trees. She turned her eyes back to the front of the room and saw that Ms. Gardner, their English teacher, was still correcting papers silently at her desk.

Toby was supposed to be reading a short story by Jack Finny about some guy who went out onto a ledge for some stupid piece of paper and got stuck out there. But right now, Toby would have given anything to be out on a window ledge looking down at the world.

The loud scuffing of Ms. Gardner's chair brought Toby's attention sharply around to the front of the room again. Ms. Gardner looked at the clock and said, "We've got about ten minutes left before the end of class and I would like to hand back writing assignments from last week."

She lifted a thick stack of papers from the corner of her desk. "Some of these papers are quite good and still others of you seem to be doing your best to stifle your imaginations. For those of you still struggling with the concept of good creative writing, I would like to read one of the better essays."

Andy looked over at Jane and winked. Surely, if Ms. Gardner was going to read one of the essays it would be Jane's. She was by far the best writer in the sophomore class, maybe even at Canby Hall. Of course, Andy realized she might be a little prejudiced.

Ms. Gardner began to read an essay entitled, "The Disney Disaster." The essay was about a vacation a family had taken that began with high hopes and ended in chaos and comic disaster. The class laughed out loud at the descriptive passages that almost took the reader inside the cramped and over-crowded car.

Andy looked across the room to Jane. She had no idea that Jane had such a sense of humor. She smiled broadly at Jane who returned her smile with a shrug of her shoulders and a quizzical expression.

Could that possibly mean that Jane hadn't written the story? Maybe she had some competition after all!

Ms. Gardner finished the story. "Now you

can see what a pleasure it is to read some of your work. I only hope those of you who are continuing to turn in mediocre work, will be encouraged to try harder on your upcoming assignment which is due one week from today."

She heard a few groans and put her hand up in a signal to be quiet. "I realize this coming weekend is open house, but you have plenty of time to get started and the essay only has to be three pages. I feel there is ample time to get it completed if you get busy right away."

She turned and wrote on the board behind her. "The Friendships I Have Known." Toby rolled her eyes toward the ceiling. It was no wonder she continued to get C's on all the writing assignments. Gardner had about as much imagination as her horse Max, when it came to selecting topics. Then she reconsidered. If given a chance, and having the ability to write it down, Max might even come up with something better.

"Well, I want to get these back to you before the bell rings. By the way, the story you all found so amusing today was written by Penelope Vanderark."

Everyone looked in Penny's direction. Toby's eyes traveled past Penny and settled on Jane. She saw the look of surprise on her face. There was something else there too. Was it a look of jealousy?

Bringing her eyes back to the middle of the room, Toby thought Penny, herself, appeared flushed with embarrassment. She almost looked like she wanted to climb under her desk and wait out the rest of the period there.

It wouldn't have been a long wait. The bell rang just as Ms. Gardner handed Toby back her essay with an unsightly red C+ scribbled across the front. Toby stuffed it inside her folder. It wasn't her fault she had never taken "A Memorable Family Vacation." Dumb essay topic anyway.

Andy had overtaken Penny by the door of the main building and was all but slapping her on the back with praise for her wonderful essay and her talented writing ability.

"But it's terrific," Andy said. "Surely, you know that? It's so natural and so funny. I just can't believe that all this time you've been telling me you don't have any talent and here you are a future . . ." Her mind went blank and she couldn't think of any great women comedy writers.

"Erma Bombeck," Toby supplied coming up beside the two of them.

"That's right. You could make a fortune on that sense of humor alone."

By then Jane had joined them and the four girls walked slowly back toward Baker House. Penny laughed nervously. "You guys are putting me on. No one would want to read a silly little story like that."

"Not only would they read it, there are magazines that would pay money for it."

"I don't believe it. It might be all right to read to a sophomore English class, but it's not good enough to print."

"Try it," Andy said. "Submit your story to the *Canby Hall Journal* and see what happens."

"I never heard of it," Penny said. "There is no *Canby Hall Journal*."

"Yes there is," Andy said.

"Then how come I've never seen it?"

"Because it's only published once a year. Tell her about it, Jane."

Jane, who up to now had been pretty quiet, looked at Andy, a touch of irritation on her face. The *Canby Hall Journal* had been her project. She really didn't want to have to share it anymore than Andy would have wanted to share her dance floor with anyone. But what could she do now?

"It's a literary magazine," Jane said informatively. "It comes out once a year and features the best writers in the school. My creative writing class is submitting articles early next week."

"See?" Penny said. "If a whole creative writing class is submitting their best work, what chance have I got?"

"But the story's great. Tell her Jane." Andy gave Jane a pleading look.

"It is good," Jane said. And it was! It wasn't

fair that she had spent days on her submission and it lacked the life that Penny seemed to put into her story so naturally. There were only so many places in the magazine and she was afraid if it came down to a decision between her article on the beauty of the New England spring or Penny's memorable family vacation to Disneyworld, she knew which one she would select.

When they got to Baker House, Jane and Toby went on up to the room. Andy took Penny by the arm and steered her toward a bench beneath a giant shade tree. She wasn't giving up so easy on her friend.

"Look, don't you see that what you've got here is a future?" Andy said pointing to the folder in Penny's hand.

"Future what?"

"You don't have to go through Vassar or Smith marking time. You can major in journalism and become something."

"I already know what my major is going to be," Penny said, a smile breaking at the corners of her mouth.

"You do?"

"I plan to get a degree in M.R.S." She smiled triumphantly. "That way I can write little stories, whenever I want, and if I'm married, I won't have to worry about anyone else liking them. They'll be just for me."

"But why write them just for yourself. What about other people?"

"They can write their own." Penny shrugged and got to her feet.

"But there are people, people like me, who couldn't write anything that great if their life depended on it. And your stories are funny and good, and they should be shared with them."

"Okay. Here." Penny said. She reached into her English folder and withdrew the story. She extended her hand toward Andy. "Now I'm sharing." She beamed a radiant smile at Andy.

"But don't you want to keep it?"

"No. I have them lying all over the place and stuffed in drawers and packed in old boxes. Besides, I can always write more."

"That's what I'm telling you," Andy said. She got to her feet and started into the building with Penny. "You have a gift. If you have these everywhere, you obviously love to write and you should be doing more of it."

"Look, Andy," Penny said, stopping at the top of the stairs. "I appreciate what you're doing, but I'm not interested in a career. I'm not like y'all. I could never make it on my own."

Andy watched Penny go into Baker House and looked down at the story she held in her hand. She sat on the top step and read it again. It was as funny the second time as it had been when Ms. Gardner had read it to them.

Suddenly she slapped her knee with the

manuscript. Penny might not be willing to submit the manuscript, but that didn't mean that she couldn't. After all, Penny had given it to her, and she should be able to do whatever she wanted with it. She jumped to her feet and nearly flew up the stairs to her room.

Andy burst into the room with excitement. Jane and Toby, who were sitting on Jane's bed talking to one another, looked up abruptly when the door banged loudly against the wall when Andy charged into the room.

"Guess what," she said breathlessly waving the manuscript in her hand, "Penny gave me this story."

"That's nice," Jane said unenthusiastically.

"Don't you get it?" Andy said coming into the room and closing the door behind her. "She wouldn't even try to submit her story to the *Journal* no matter how hard I tried to talk her into it, but she didn't say *I* couldn't do it for her."

"Maybe that's not such a good idea," Jane said.

"Why?"

"Well, I would think if she was interested in the *Journal*, she would submit the story herself."

"I think she's afraid."

"Of what?" Toby asked.

"That maybe people won't like it and then they won't like her anymore. She cares about pleasing people. I mean, why else would she let her parents plan her life for her?"

"All our parents plan our lives somewhat," Jane pointed out.

"Yeah, but Penny's different."

"You can say that again," Toby muttered.

"We listen to our parents and then we still do what we think is best. Like my coming to school here. If I'd listened to my parents, I'd still be back in Chicago. Sometimes you have to take a chance, and I don't think Penny will take that chance unless we push her into it."

Jane got up from the bed and went over to her desk. She began to clear away the stack of paper on top of it. Andy came over next to her. She set the manuscript on the desk next to Jane. "Well, read it again and see what you think. Maybe I'm wrong about it. Maybe it's nothing out of the ordinary."

Jane picked up a ball point pen and began to doodle absently on a sheet of paper as she read. It was good. And she hated Penny for it.

Sighing, Jane set the manuscript aside and looked over at Andy who sat expectantly on the bed next to Jane's desk waiting for her reply. "It's good," Jane said. She turned the sheet of paper over that she had been drawing on and saw it was the rough draft for her own story. She began to reread it. Suddenly, her own writing seemed flat. It didn't seem to sound nearly as good to her as it had yesterday.

It wasn't fair, Jane decided. Up till then, it was okay for Penny to be cute and bubbly because Jane had considered her an airhead and nobody to worry about. Why, even the other night when they had gone to hear Cary play, and Jane had mentioned how cute Penny was, Cary had said she was all right, but she wasn't his type. He liked the kind of girl with whom you could have an intelligent conversation. Looking at the story on her desk, Jane began to realize that maybe Penny wasn't as empty-headed as she would have them all believe.

But even worse than that was the fact that Penny really didn't care about the *Journal.* It didn't matter to her if she ever got her story published or not. To Jane it was probably the most important thing that would happen to her all year. She would never be able to live with the disappointment, if her story got rejected to make room for Penny's and she knew that Penny never cared in the first place.

Jane got up from her desk. "Go ahead and submit it if you want. You're taking a real chance though. If that article shows up in the *Journal,* Penny may not be as overjoyed as you think she'll be. She might find self-confidence, but you might lose a friend."

Andy slipped quietly down the hall of the third floor in the deserted main building. She had carried the manuscript around with her all day. Twice she had almost broached the subject of the *Journal* with Penny, but both times something happened and she backed down.

She had nearly asked Ms. Gardner to submit it for her, but if she said no it might only make things more complicated. As it was, she might be able to leave the story in the journalism room and people would think Penny had left it there herself.

Andy really believed that Penny would be pleased if the story was published, but the hard knot in her stomach told her that maybe Jane was right. There was a chance that Penny really believed the best she could hope for was being someone's wife, which wasn't all bad. Andy wanted to get married some day too. But a person could still be married and fulfill their dreams. Penny had talent and it seemed a shame no one else knew about it.

Andy pulled the door of the journalism room open and peeked inside. The setting sun left the room bathed in a soft orange glow that settled on the silent typewriters sitting beneath their dust covers. She tiptoed across the room and set the story on the desk by the back wall. The note she attached to it read: "I would like to submit this story for consideration in the *Canby Hall Journal.*"

CHAPTER NINE

Sitting at the cafeteria table with Toby and Andy, Jane carefully lifted the steaming mixture of floury white sauce and thinly sliced pink beef to her nose. She sniffed delicately. "Do you think it's safe to eat this?"

Toby smiled broadly. "Of course, it is." She thrust a heaping forkful of the creamed beef on toast into her mouth.

"I think you asked the wrong person," Dee said, setting her tray on the table beside Jane. She pulled the chair back and sat down. "How is everything going?"

"Great," Andy said with enthusiasm. "We're getting all set for this weekend. How about you?"

Dee threw back her head, flinging her long, blonde hair to one side. "I think Maggie needs to be a social director when she grows up. She's done nothing but make plans since this whole thing came up."

"And it's a good thing I have," Maggie put in. "Otherwise, we'd be spending Saturday night sitting in Baker House staring at each other."

"That's not entirely true." Dee gave them a wink. "I thought of several things we could do. It's not my fault we can't go surfing in the Atlantic right now or plan a beach party on the shores of the creek."

"Those sound like great activities," Toby laughed.

"Well, they're the only ones I know how to plan."

"We're going to keep it simple," Jane said. "We thought that would give us time to talk and that way, we could answer any questions they might have."

"Yeah," Andy said. "And like Dee pointed out, there really isn't a lot to do around here that isn't simple. We're not exactly a metropolis."

"Well, I don't know about you guys," Maggie commented, "But I just can't wait."

Jane had finally given up on her chipped beef surprise, and she pushed her chair back from the table. "Well, if this weekend is going to be any fun, I'd better get back to the room and finish my homework. I still haven't even started that essay for English."

"Don't remind me," Toby said, pulling herself to her feet. She had tried to write the paper several times, but it always came out sounding boring or musty. Why didn't Ms. Gardner let them pick their own topics? That way she could write about things like her horse, or the wide open spaces of Texas that she knew like the back of her hand. But no, they had to write about memorable family vacations and friendships they'd known. Yuk.

Toby sat at her desk and pulled at her ear as she tried to make sense out of the latest attempt at her English essay. She finally crumpled it up and took aim before carefully shooting it in a perfect arc toward the garbage can near the door. It dropped in and she said, "Two points."

Andy and Jane looked up briefly from their own desks. "Toby, you really need to work on your attention span," Jane said with exasperation. "It's so difficult to concentrate when you're over there doing imitations of Willie Mays."

"Who?"

"Willie Mays, the basketball player."

"Willie Mays played baseball and it was years ago," Toby said.

"Oh. Well, whatever you're doing over there, it's driving me crazy."

"Sorry." Toby got up. "I'll just take a walk down the hall. Maybe when I get back I'll be able to think."

Jane almost came back with some retort about needing a much longer walk than that before she would be able to do much thinking, but there was no need to have an argument just before open house this weekend. And besides, she'd probably be sorry if she let herself say anything so mean. After all, there was nothing dumb about Toby. She knew her priorities. Studying just wasn't one of them.

Toby walked along the hall glancing into the rooms where the doors were open. She saw Penny sitting cross-legged on an unmade bed, clothes and books scattered all around her. She held some kind of tray on her lap that she was writing on. Penny sucked at the end of her pencil and wrinkled her brow as she reread whatever it was she had just written. Suddenly, she sensed Toby standing in the doorway and looked up.

"Hi, what you doing?" Penny asked.

"Just taking a short walk to clear my head." Toby leaned against the door jamb.

"Want to come in?" Penny asked as she tried to untangle herself from the crumpled bedding to get up. In the process, she caught her foot in the twisted sheet, and grabbed at the foot of the bed as she slid to the floor pulling the sheet, and all the books resting on it, to the floor beside her. She looked at Toby and collapsed into a fit of giggles. "That'll teach me not to make my bed."

Toby came into the room and helped her up. Penny knelt down to untangle the sheet from her foot. She said sheepishly, "I guess I sort of got wrapped up in it."

Toby smiled at Penny, then bent over and picked up the tray Penny had been writing on. "What are you doing here?" She looked down and saw Penny's essay on friendship was clipped to the board by a large spring clip. The paper had been crossed over and re-written. Arrows darted out in wide arcs that probably meant she was supposed to rearrange those places. "Your essay for English, huh?"

Before Toby could read what was written, Penny quickly took it from her hand. "Thanks," she muttered in what appeared to be genuine embarrassment.

"I haven't got much of a start on mine," Toby sighed. She almost sat down, but didn't see a clear spot so she settled for leaning against the desk.

"I know what you mean." Penny set the essay on the floor and lifted the balled up sheets back onto the bed. "I've started this stupid thing over about four times."

"Well, you've got a lot more on paper than I do. Of course, you're a lot better writer than I am," Toby said, remembering the essay Ms. Gardner had shared with the class on Monday.

"Oh, I'm not that good," Penny said. A self-conscious smile crept across her pretty face.

"You sounded pretty good to me."

Penny turned and grabbed at some of the papers on the floor and crumpled them into a ball. "I don't know why she read that stupid story in class. It's been nothing but trouble ever since." She shoved the paper into the already overflowing garbage can.

Toby watched Penny with bewilderment. Penny seemed to enjoy being the center of attention when she was made to look like a fool. When people were laughing at her, she didn't mind at all. In fact, she encouraged them to laugh when she told those silly stories about all the dumb things she did. But now that she had a chance for real admiration, she seemed embarrassed about the whole thing.

"It's just that now everyone thinks I'm some great writer and I'm not. I like to tell stories, that's all," she said feebly. "Believe me, I'm not the next Agatha Christie. And I know she just wrote mysteries."

"Well, you're a lot closer to it than I am," Toby said.

Toby straightened up and started for the door. "Well, I guess I'd better get on back to my room so you can finish that and I can get mine started."

"Good luck," Penny said. "Let me know if I can help you." Toby smiled at Penny and Penny smiled back. For the first time since they'd met, Toby thought there might be a chance that she could get to like Penny.

Coming back into the room, Toby saw things hadn't changed much. Jane was still hunched over her desk scribbling furiously, while Andy sat engrossed in some book she was studying. She went across the room and dropped onto her bed.

"I thought you were going to work on that essay tonight," Jane said.

"I'm still thinking." Toby put her hands behind her head and studied the tea bag hanging above her bed. Now *that* would make an interesting essay. She had her reasons for that tea bag and some day, she might just put them all down on paper for the world to know about. But right now, she'd settle for some idea of how to begin that stupid paper on friendship.

Toby was rolling off the bed to get started when Maggie knocked lightly on the door. "Jane, Cary called. He wants you to call him back as soon as you can. It's important." Jane got up from her desk and left the room.

Maggie sat down. "How's the homework coming?"

"Don't ask," Toby said. She went to her desk and dropped into the chair.

"Well, you looked like you were studying real hard when I came in." A smile crept onto her face and the two of them laughed. Andy looked up from her book. "Sorry," Maggie said.

"I need a break anyway." Andy closed her book and stretched her arms high above her head as she leaned back in her chair.

While the three of them became engaged in a lively conversation about the upcoming weekend, Jane stood in the phone booth downstairs, holding the receiver and listening to Cary tell her about his big plans for Saturday night.

"When Grant called and said their drummer had sprained his wrist and couldn't play for the dance Saturday night, I wondered what that had to do with me. I'm no drummer."

"Does he want Erik to play?" Erik was the drummer for Ambulance. "I thought that might be it, too, but then I wondered why he just didn't call Erik himself. That was when he told me he was hoping we could take the gig for them."

"You mean play at the Westfield Inn?" Jane asked. She hadn't been there herself, but several of the girls had. It was about the classiest place around without going into Boston. The Westfield was where a lot of the senior girls took their dates before the big graduation dance. It was a definite cut above the places in Greenleaf. It was too bad she couldn't take the new girls there this weekend. Then suddenly she had a great idea.

"Look, we have that open house Saturday night. Why don't we meet you guys there and listen to the band?"

"Well, that's sort of why I'm calling." Jane felt her heart racing. "See, I really want you to come, but it's a private party and they might not take to me inviting five girls to crash it, but I'm sure they wouldn't say anything if there was only one girl." Jane hesitated.

"I could pick you up about seven, and that would give us time to have dinner at the Westfield before the band started warming up."

Jane thought about the runny chipped beef they'd been served for dinner. It had been a long time since she'd had a good meal. It would be so fun to get dressed up nice and go to have a lovely dinner, then sit back and watch Cary and the band play.

Briefly she thought about Toby and Andy and their plans for this weekend. But they really didn't need her. There were only two girls coming in and she'd be with them all afternoon. There was no need for her to give up her Saturday night as well. She was sure they'd understand.

Cary took Jane's silence on the other end to mean that she was thinking about saying no. "Come on, Jane," he pleaded. "Think of it. My first big break and I want you there to share it with me. What do you say?"

"Why not?"

"Great! I'll pick you up about seven. Oh, man, this is going to be totally awesome. You wait and see."

Jane's excitement seemed to vanish along with her courage when she put the phone back on the hook. It was one thing to tell

Cary she was going, but it would be another to break the news to Toby and Andy. But then she thought of her two roommates and knew they'd do the same thing if they had a chance. It was just some silly little open house. No one was going to care if she went to hear Cary's band instead.

CHAPTER TEN

Jane pushed the door open and saw the three girls sitting around talking about this weekend. Was that all anyone could think about? She felt a momentary stab of nerves before walking bravely over to her bed and sitting down.

"Was that Cary?" Andy asked.

"Uh huh," Jane said. She took her pencil and pretended to make changes and rewrites on her essay which had been lying next to the bed. She didn't want to talk to them about Cary until Maggie left and they could discuss it alone.

But Maggie didn't look like she had any intention of leaving though. She talked on enthusiastically about the open house while Jane chewed on the eraser of her pencil and wondered how she was going to break the news to her roommates.

They heard a whooshing sound in the hall

and all three girls looked up. Dee slid past the door in her stocking feet. She grabbed the door jamb and came to an abrupt stop. She looked in and smiled. She saw Maggie on the bed. "I've been looking everywhere for you."

"Well, I've been right here. What do you need?"

"Nothing. I just finished my homework and I got bored, so I came looking for you."

"Well, unfortunately, I still haven't finished my homework, so I guess I better get out of here or I'll never get it done." Maggie got up from the chair, and Dee followed her toward the door. "It's been great talking to you, but if I don't get this paper written, I'll end up spending this weekend thinking about *it* instead of open house."

"That's doubtful," Dee said.

The door closed behind them and Toby said, "What did Cary have to say?"

"Not much except his band is playing at the Westfield this weekend," Jane said with a sly smile.

"The Westfield?" Andy jumped to her feet. "Oh, Jane, aren't you just dying?"

"Well of course, I am," Jane said, getting to her feet, no longer able to control her excitement. "The drummer of the other band that was supposed to play for this big private party sprained his wrist, and they want Cary's band to play instead. Isn't that great?"

"When's this going to happen?" Andy said.

"Saturday night."

"What a shame you won't be able to go." Toby shook her head.

"Yeah, but wouldn't it be great if all of us could go hear Cary play? And at the Westfield, no less." Andy said. "That would really be some memorable way to spend Saturday night, huh?" The note of hope in her voice was unmistakable.

"Well, actually, I suggested that," Jane said. She saw the look of excitement that danced across Andy's face. "But Cary said since this is some big private party, he didn't think he would ever be able to get away with smuggling all five of us in."

"What a shame," Andy said. "It's too bad you have to miss it."

"Oh, I knew you'd feel that way," Jane said with enthusiasm as she got to her feet and hugged Andy. "I just knew you'd understand."

Andy knitted her brow in confusion. "Understand? What will I understand?"

"Why I have to go with Cary on Saturday night."

Toby jumped to her feet. "You what?"

"But what about open house?" Andy said at the same time. "All the plans we made?"

"You guys don't need me." Jane said. "There's only two girls coming in, and besides, I'll be with you all afternoon."

"Well, don't put yourself out or anything, Jane," Toby said.

"I don't get it, what are you guys so mad about? So I won't be there to eat pizza and see a movie with all of you, big deal."

"Yes, it *is* a big deal!" Andrea said getting to her feet. "We've been planning this thing for weeks and now you just decide you're not coming because Cary calls you up and invites you to do something else."

"That's not so," Jane fumed.

"Oh, isn't it? Why didn't you tell him that you had something else planned?"

"He knew about open house, but — "

"But he figured that it didn't matter," Andy said.

"Obviously he was right," Toby observed.

"You guys are twisting things all around," Jane said almost in tears. "It's not fair."

"I'll tell you what's not fair," Andy said. "Making plans and letting us think you really wanted to be with us and then deserting us because a date with Cary sounds like more fun."

"What's the use?" Jane said hotly. "You just refuse to try and understand, but if you were the one with a chance to go to the Westfield, I'm sure the choice would be a lot easier."

"That's right, it would be," Andy said indignantly, "I wouldn't even consider it."

Jane stared at Andy for a tense moment and then looked toward Toby to be greeted by an equally cold stare. No help there. She was alone in this.

Well, who needed them anyway? She turned abruptly and went out the door and down to the laundry room where she found a quiet corner where she could think and be angry.

What did Toby and Andy know about anything? Neither of them *had* a steady boyfriend so they didn't understand what she was going through. She hardly ever got to see Cary and she saw them all the time.

Besides, what was so big about having dinner in Greenleaf and seeing some crummy movie? Why should she give up a wonderful evening and a delicious dinner, just to sit around and talk to a bunch of girls? She would make sure to make a good impression on Saturday afternoon. It wouldn't matter if she spent the evening with them. She was sure that if she explained why she wasn't going to be around Saturday night, the new girls would understand. And probably a lot better than her own roommates did.

As she sat in the corner of the laundry room smelling the powdered detergents, she came to realize that jealousy was probably what was wrong with her roommates. They were the ones with the problem, not her. She wouldn't let it ruin her big night out with Cary.

Jane came back to the room to a chilly

reception. Andy was lying on her bed listening to her Walkman. She looked up from the book she was reading and then slowly lowered her eyes again.

Toby continued to scratch at the sheet of paper in front of her like she was sincerely trying to write something. Jane knew it was all a ruse. They were both ignoring her. Well, she could play that game too.

Jane sat at her own desk and took out her paper on friendship. She looked at the first lines she'd written about the qualities of a friend and wadded the paper up in anger. She drew out a clean sheet and began to write.

"Friends are people who understand you and don't judge you for doing something you really want to do even if it means going against what they want." She read it over to herself and continued to write. She would write down all her feelings and then leave her essay lying around where they were sure to see it, and she wouldn't have to worry about talking to them if they wanted to be childish about the whole thing.

A glorious sunny day greeted the girls from outside their window the next morning. It was a contrast from the gloom that hung inside Room 407. Jane got her towel and padded off to the shower without a word.

Toby looked over at Andy who was lost in deep thought as she made her bed. "Can you believe that Jane would just desert us like that?" Toby asked.

Andy looked up from her housekeeping. "Maybe she's had second thoughts. We were pretty rough on her last night. I bet if we gave her another chance, she'd change her mind."

"You really think so?"

"Sure, I do. She probably feels rotten and she's waiting for us to bring the subject up again so she can tell us she made a mistake."

"If you say so," Toby said, but the sound of her voice said that she was not at all convinced that Andrea Cord was right.

Jane came back from the shower wearing a flowing pink bathrobe and a towel wrapped tightly around her head. She stopped near her bed and unwrapped the towel, shaking her long blonde hair. Without so much as a word to either of them, she went over to the closet and began getting dressed.

"About last night," Andy said hesitantly. Jane looked up expectantly, but didn't say anything. "Toby and I thought you might . . ."

"Might what?" Jane said coming toward them holding her skirt in her hand.

"Well, that you might want to . . ."

While Andy searched for a delicate way to state it, Toby blurted out from across the room. "To wise up and come with us instead," Toby finished.

"Who could resist such a delicate invitation?" Andy said looking abruptly at Toby then back to Jane.

"I thought we had settled this last night," Jane said. "I feel really bad about not going with you guys on Saturday, but I still say if you had the chance you'd do the same thing."

"The whole idea of this weekend is to show the new girls the kind of friendships we have here. Special friendships that come from living with a person and caring about them like a family," Andy said.

"Well, then it ought to be easy for my *sisters* to understand that another chance like this might not come along for ages." Jane was still holding her skirt in the hand that she shook in their direction.

"Well, neither will this weekend."

"That's not true. We've still got two more years at Canby Hall and lots of time to make friends and memories together," Jane pleaded. "I mean, the thing is, you guys are my roommates, and we can be together whenever we want to."

"I wouldn't be so sure," Toby said.

"What's that supposed to mean?" Jane asked.

"Well, maybe when you're ready to be with us, we may not be ready for you." Toby picked up her books and went toward the door. Andy silently gathered her things from the desk and followed her out. Jane stood in the center of the sunlit room and felt a chill steal over her.

Chapter Eleven

Andy and Toby came out of Baker House together. The early morning sun felt warm against their faces. Neither of them paid much attention to the beautiful spring day, however. They both had other things on their minds.

"I can't believe Jane would desert us like that," Toby said with obvious annoyance in her voice.

"I guess that's because she just takes us for granted. She figures we're always going to be around for her. She probably knows that even if she goes out with Cary, we'll still be her roommates, but if she goes out with us, he may not keep on being her boyfriend."

"So? What kind of boyfriend is it that expects you to break commitments with your friends just because he snaps his fingers?" Toby fumed.

They came into the nearly deserted cafeteria. Toby went through the line picking up dry cereal, milk, toast, and even taking a chance on some runny looking scrambled eggs.

"You're going to eat that?"

"Sure."

"You must have the toughest stomach at Canby Hall," Andy muttered. She looked up at the girl behind the counter. "Just toast for me, thanks."

They had their choice of tables. The two of them went toward the row of windows on the east side and sat in the warm sunshine. Maggie and Dee entered just as they sat down. The two girls went through the serving line not taking much more than Andy had and then made their way over to the table where Andy and Toby were sitting.

"I can't believe you're actually eating that," Maggie said.

"Yeah, I usually serve it, and I wouldn't be caught dead eating it," Dee said. Dee worked in the cafeteria and that was actually how she and Toby had met. Dee had accidentally sprinkled pepper on some doughnuts one morning and the supervisor was about to fire Dee. Toby told her that she had asked for it that way. She had even taken a bite of the thing. It had nearly gagged her, but it had saved Dee's job. They'd been friends ever since.

"Yeah, how come you're not working this morning?" Toby asked.

"Took the day off to get ready for this weekend," Dee said. "I don't want to miss a thing."

"This open house is the biggest thing that's happened here all year. I can't imagine anybody wanting to miss it."

"Jane does," Toby said.

"What?" Dee asked.

"Well, Jane has decided it will be more fun to go hear Cary's band play then spend Saturday night with us, so she's not coming with us tomorrow night."

The girls didn't see Penny come up behind their table. Her soft voice startled both Toby and Andy when she said, "I can't believe it."

"Penny, have a seat," Andy said.

"I stopped by your room, and Jane was sitting on her bed looking like she didn't have a friend in the world."

"She doesn't," Toby said.

"I asked her if she wanted to come over to the cafeteria with me, but she said she wasn't eating this morning. Now I think I know why."

"Well, it's her own fault. She's the one who decided she'd rather be with Cary than us, so she can just have him," Toby said.

"Is that going to louse up your plans for tomorrow?" Penny asked with genuine concern.

"No, one person more or less won't make any difference," Andy said. "It's just that it would have been nice to have had all three of us together since togetherness is what this whole weekend is supposed to be about."

Penny sat down beside Andy and Andy's face lit up as she turned to face her. "Hey, you still want to come along tomorrow night?"

Penny wrinkled her brow. "How come?"

"Because we'd love to have you and you'd be lots of fun. What do you say?"

"Well, sure, if you don't think Ms. Allardyce will mind."

"Of course, she won't. It's all settled then, right?" Andy got to her feet and picked up her tray. The others did the same and the five girls walked out of the cafeteria and toward first period.

Jane was already in class sitting along the wall looking thoroughly dejected. She saw the girls come in and looked toward the front of the room.

They took their seats. Andy and Toby did their best to ignore Jane, but Penny managed to give her an encouraging nod. Jane seemed grateful for the attention and smiled briefly at her.

Jane didn't hear a thing that went on all period. She might as well have stayed in bed. All she could think about was her dilemma. If she went with the girls, she would miss the chance of a lifetime, and if she went with Cary, she might lose her best friends.

Then she would reason that she wasn't

going to lose anybody. They might be mad at her for a little while, but they'd get over it. After all, they were her friends, even if they weren't speaking to her right now.

As the bell rang, Jane began gathering her things. She ended up at the door the same time as Toby. They looked at each other for a minute in cold silence before Toby pushed past her and out the door.

Jane thought about skipping lunch too, but after eating hardly any dinner the night before and missing breakfast, she thought she would collapse if she missed out on lunch as well. Besides, she had as much right as anybody to go to the cafeteria. After all, why was she acting so guilty? She hadn't done anything that terrible.

Jane took her tuna salad and iced tea and started for a corner table, but then she saw Maggie and Dee and changed directions. She walked over to their table.

"Mind if I sit down?"

"Course not," Dee said. "How's it going?"

"Fine."

"I understand you got a hot date tomorrow night," Dee said just as Maggie kicked her under the table. "Ow!" Dee yelped looking sharply at Maggie who glared back at her.

Jane looked at both of them. "I see you've been talking to my roommates." She picked at her tuna salad with her fork. It wasn't bad enough that they were mad at her, now they had to drag everyone else into it too.

"It's no big deal, really," Jane assured them. "We've only got the two girls, and I'm sure that Toby and Andy can entertain them without any problem."

"Well, they won't have too," Dee said.

"Why not?"

"Because Penny's going along to take your place, and she's a regular one-person entertainment factory."

"Well, that's good," Jane said with forced cheerfulness. But she didn't feel so good about it. It certainly hadn't taken them long to find a replacement for her. Just the other day, Toby had practically insulted Penny when Toby'd all but told her they didn't want her tagging along with them. How quickly people change, Jane thought.

The rest of the afternoon passed in a blur. Jane went to her classes but didn't retain a thing that had been said by any of her teachers. Every time she looked around she saw girls making last-minute plans for the weekend.

Coming out of class Friday afternoon, she noticed the grounds committee working on the decorations and the welcome banner. Bunches of girls were weeding flower beds and tying ribbons around the trees in school colors. Everywhere she looked were reminders of the weekend she had decided to skip out on.

But then she got angry with herself and reminded herself that she wasn't really skipping out on anything. She would be there all day tomorrow. She'd attend the luncheon and the afternoon games. Actually, she was going to miss very little of the planned activities. So, she asked herself, why didn't that make her feel any better?

The girls took their places in the auditorium for the general meeting to go over final plans for the next day's activities. The hum in the room grew steadily louder as the number of girls increased.

Jane sat stiffly at the end of the row and tried to block out all the excited chatter around her. The more she thought about it, she decided the more ridiculous it seemed that the whole school was in an uproar over this dumb open house.

Ms. Allardyce stepped to the microphone and the girls began to quiet down. She tapped it once to be sure that it was on and then she began to speak.

"Well! Tomorrow is the big day. The girls are due here about nine-thirty in the morning. We'll meet on the lawn in front of the main building. It would be nice if you had signs to hold up with the names of your girls if you are hosting so that it will be easier to locate you in all the commotion."

She put her half-glasses on the tip of her

nose and began reading the schedule. "After everyone has a chance to meet, we'll move to this room and begin with a few general comments about the school's history."

There were a few soft groans and moans which went unnoticed by the headmistress. The school's history was her favorite subject. Every student had heard the lecture at least once, and most of them had heard it a lot more than that.

"We'll talk about the agenda for the day, and then you'll be free to tour the campus. While you're showing the girls around, I'll be visiting with parents and answering any questions that they may have. We'll all meet in the Dining Hall at 11:30."

"Well, that does it," Dee leaned over and whispered to the girls. "If we feed them in our cafeteria, they'll probably all die of food poisoning before they can get enrolled."

Some of the girls around her giggled softly, but not softly enough. Patrice Allardyce heard them and looked up sharply from her notes.

"To continue on," she said looking right at the girls, "the afternoon will offer a variety of events which you may take part in. Some of you may wish to use the pool or the tennis courts. There will be a baseball game at 1:00 for any of you wanting to play. The coaches have asked that you please sign up in the morning if you think you might be interested so that they can organize the teams. I would encourage many of you to attend the choir concert at 3:00.

"The important thing is, no matter what you choose to do tomorrow, this is your chance to show them Canby Hall and all that it stands for. This is *our* school and we're proud of it. Let them see the pride and love we have here, and the school will speak for itself."

She put her glasses on the stand next to her and looked out among the girls with a broad smile. "As you can see, tomorrow is going to be a full day for all of us. I am sure you're as excited as I am. I know everything will go well. I hope you will all go back to your rooms and get a good night's sleep. I want you to be rested and ready for the big day ahead of us. Goodnight, girls."

The girls applauded politely as Ms. Allardyce picked up her glasses and her notes and left the podium. After she left, they got to their feet and began shuffling toward the door. There were several conversations taking place at once. The room was a hum of noise and excitement. The only person who felt apart from it all was Jane, who was trying to work her way toward the door so she could go back to the room and wallow in her self-imposed exile.

CHAPTER TWELVE

Toby rolled over, opened one sleepy eye and looked out the window. The sky provided a brilliant blue background for the bright new green leaves dancing slowly outside the glass to the gentle motion of the early morning breeze.

Toby lifted her sheet and got out of bed. She knelt near the window with her arms resting on the sill and studied the still-sleeping campus around her. The lush greenery of the East Coast was such a contrast from her native Texas flatlands! Though she had always been able to appreciate the beauty of it, she didn't think she'd ever grow to love it as much as the scruffy mesquite bushes that sprang up at will across the deceptively barren-looking Texas plains.

"What're you looking at?" Andrea whispered from across the room.

Toby turned and saw she was leaning up on

one elbow, her head resting on her hand. "Nothing." Toby got to her feet feeling somewhat self-conscious at being caught daydreaming about home. "Looks like it's going to be a great day for open house."

"Yeah?" Andy threw back her covers and came across the room to sit next to Toby on her bed. Andy turned and looked back over her shoulder at Jane who was still sleeping soundly. "I've been thinking," she whispered.

"About what?"

"Well, maybe we're making too much about this whole thing where Jane is concerned."

"Are you kidding me?"

"It's just that I think it's important that we try to get along today. What good will it do to show our friendship if all we show them is how good we can ignore each other?"

"I don't know," Toby said hesitantly.

"Look, I still don't think it's right that she's deserting us, but we need to forget about tonight and concentrate on today."

"Maybe you're right." Toby got to her feet. "I guess we'd better hit the showers before the rest of the world wakes up and things are mass chaos down there."

"Be right there."

Toby went down the hall toward the showers while Andy looked for her shampoo. When Toby came through the door, she was more than a little surprised to find that several other girls had had the same idea she did and were already in the showers. She leaned against one of the sinks to wait.

"Excuse me," a girl that Toby thought was named Nicole said to her. "Are you using this?" She pointed her toothbrush toward the sink that Toby was leaning on.

"No, go ahead." She stepped out just as Andrea came through the door. "Looks like we weren't the only ones up early today."

They stopped by Penny's room on the way back to their own room. Penny was still curled into a ball beneath her lavender blanket. "You going with us today, sleeping beauty?" Andy asked.

Penny rolled over and looked up in surprise at the two people standing at her bedside. "Oh, my gosh," she said sitting up and letting the sheet fall away from her pink baby-doll pajamas. "What time is it?"

She looked around the room anxiously while Toby glanced over at the clock near the desk. "Almost eight-thirty."

"Oh, no, this is awful. I set my alarm for seven, I know I did." She got out of bed and went across to the desk. "Oops," she said before releasing a torrent of giggles. "I set it, but I forgot to pull this little thingy back here." She held the alarm clock toward them.

"It's a good thing we stopped by," Andy said.

"Boy, you're not kidding. I just hope I can get ready in an hour." Her hand went to her near perfect hair, and Toby wondered how anyone could wake up looking so good. She usually woke up with her red curly hair going in several directions at once. Penny looked like she had just laid down. Some people had all the luck.

"I'll meet you guys back at the room," Toby said.

"I'll be right behind you," Andy called.

Toby heard the muffle of voices behind her as she went down the hall toward 407. All up and down the hall, rooms were buzzing with sound. She could hear several different radio stations playing softly in various rooms. Someone was arguing down the hall, and laughter came bursting out of the bathroom at the end of the hall.

Toby turned around in time to see Dee come flying out the door with someone's towel in her hand. Then she heard the girl calling out for Dee to bring it back. Toby smiled. This was the kind of thing the new girls should see. *This* was Canby Hall. More than the stuffy old buildings, or the town of Greenleaf, or Ms. Allardyce's lectures on Canby Hall, this was what it was all about. Living in this house with all these other girls and being able to feel a part of it.

Was she *ever* being sentimental this morning, she thought, pushing herself away from the wall and opening the door of their room. Jane was standing at the mirror trying different things with her hair. She pulled it into a long ponytail and held it up behind her. Then she moved it to the side and cocked her head critically. She dropped it around her shoulders and shook it out before taking the sides and pulling them back.

"I liked it on the side," Toby said.

Jane let go of her hair and looked over at Toby. "You talking to me?"

"Sure. Why shouldn't I be? Aren't you my roommate or did I stumble into the wrong room?" Toby pretended to survey her surroundings.

"Oh, you're up. Good." Andy said coming into the room. Jane stared at her in puzzlement. "I'm going to wear shorts. What about you guys?"

"Jeans for me probably," Toby said.

"So what else is new? How about you, Jane?"

"Well, I thought I'd wear shorts too. I mean it's such a nice day today."

Andy glanced out the window again for the second time that morning. "Yep. It sure is." She pulled out a pair of brightly colored shorts and a matching blouse and began getting dressed. Jane wasn't sure what had changed since last night, but it sure was great to have her roommates speaking to her again.

After Penny had joined them, the four girls went down on the lawn in front of the main building where everyone was to meet. They had prepared a poster with their names on it so the new girls could find them more easily. There were several girls milling around looking for someone in particular. Those were the Canby Hall girls. Other girls were milling around looking confused. Those were the new girls.

A tall slender girl with short light-brown hair that was stylishly high-lighted around her face walked up to the four girls holding up the giant welcome sign. "Andy?" She said to Penny.

"Try again," Andy said.

"*You're* Andy," she said with relief. "Thank goodness you had this sign. I didn't think there would be so many people."

"Well, since you don't have a sign, you have us at a disadvantage," Jane said.

"Oh, I'm sorry. I'm Jennie."

"And this is Jane, October, call her Toby, and Penny," Andy said.

"Wow, you all look just like I pictured you would. This is so exciting," Jennie said. "I've been wanting to come to a school like this since I was in grade school."

"How'd you find out about Canby Hall?" Jane asked.

"One day I was in the counselor's office dropping Algebra II for a theater arts class, and I saw this poster on the wall. At first I thought it was some Ivy League college and I pulled the information card to find out more about it. Then I read the brochure and saw that it was a high school. It took me the rest of the year to talk my parents into letting me come here. They're still not sold on the idea. They said they planned on having me around for two more years."

"You're a sophomore, then?" Andy asked.

"Yeah. I'm getting a late start."

"I didn't start until this last January," Penny said.

"Then I feel better."

A dark-haired girl with beautiful big brown eyes and striking good looks came over to them. "I'm April Wilson. Is this the right bunch?"

"You bet," Andy said. "I'm Andy Cord. This is Jane Barrett, Toby Houston, and Penny Vanderark." She extended a friendly hand. "Welcome to Canby Hall."

Chapter Thirteen

The girls fell into step with the flow of people headed for the main building where they were to meet with Patrice Allardyce. Toby and Andy walked with Jennie, while Penny and Jane walked with April tucked between them. With the confusion of so many people headed in the same direction, they didn't want to take a chance on getting separated from one another.

Andy found a group of empty seats toward the back of the auditorium and sidestepped her way into them. The other girls followed her lead, "excuse-me-ing" to everyone.

"You know, I think that row back there had more people in it," Toby commented. "Why didn't you pick that one so we could really get some practice at dodging feet?"

"If you wouldn't insist on wearing those stupid boots, you wouldn't have to worry about tromping on everyone's toes," Andy whispered.

"These 'stupid boots' as you call them are eel and probably cost more than ten pairs of those stupid sandals you're wearing."

"I wasn't referring to cost so much as size." Andy looked down at her own size 5 shoe.

Ms. Allardyce came onto the stage wearing a linen suit of off-white. The cranberry blouse she wore beneath it was accented by an antique cameo at the neck. She was followed by the faculty and the house mothers, all of whom were suitably dressed for the morning's presentation. Even Meredith, who had given up her original strict housemother image for a casual look, had dragged out one of her old suits and pulled her hair back.

The commotion in the room began to die down, but several conversations were still buzzing when Ms. Allardyce stepped to the microphone. "Excuse me, girls. Excuse me." She tapped the mike once to be sure it was on while she waited for silence. She was not accustomed to waiting for anything, but several of the new girls were excited to be there, and continued whisperings could be heard.

"I'm waiting." Ms. Allardyce looked out over the group of girls gathered in front of her. The room became deathly quiet. "That's better," she said with a satisfied smile. "I'd like to take this opportunity to welcome you all to Canby Hall this morning and tell you that we hope you are as excited to be here as we are to have you."

She looked around the room, welcoming everyone with a warm smile. "Before you begin the day's festivities, I'd like to begin by telling you a little bit about Canby Hall." She picked up her reading glasses and set them on her nose.

"The school was founded in 1897, when Julia Canby, an only child of industrialist Horace Canby, died of fever. The land you will be visiting today would have been her inheritance, had she lived.

"The family home, which you'll see later on this morning, that faces the park with the wishing pool, became the home of the residing headmistress and that is where I live now."

"I know right where that is," Penny whispered to April. "I can tell you all about it."

"She's even had tea there," Jane said softly breaking into a smile which the two of them shared, stirring April's curiosity.

"The school opened with just thirty girls," Ms. Allardyce was saying. "The main building where you are now and Baker House were the first buildings on campus."

While Patrice Allardyce continued with her informative lecture about Canby Hall that made her sound more like a tour guide than a headmistress, Toby looked around the room at the new girls. Most of them seemed to be hanging on the headmistress's every word.

There was one girl down the row and up one aisle from them that Toby thought looked really interesting. She had taken a pen out of her pocket and was drawing what appeared to be a face on her hand. Then she scrunched her fingers up so they looked like a mouth and she began to move her hand to the sound of Ms. Allardyce's voice. It looked like her hand was talking and Toby started to laugh. She felt someone kick her foot and she looked over at Jane who was giving her a dirty look.

Toby bit her lip and promised herself she would have to meet that girl before the day was over. She'd bet anything, it had been that girl's parents' idea to come to Candy Hall, and she probably was wishing she was some place else today. Well, Toby knew what that felt like, and she'd tell her so. She also knew from experience, that that girl would probably like it here if she gave it a chance.

"We have several wonderful New England activities here at Canby Hall," Ms. Allardyce was saying. "In the fall we make apple butter from the orchard's harvest and serve it on homemade bread. The maple trees to the north provide us with a wonderful opportunity to enjoy real maple syrup at the annual pancake festival. There's just so much to tell you about that I could stay up here for hours. But I'm sure that's not why you're here today.

"Without further delay, I'd like to briefly introduce our faculty to you and let you get on with today's activities." Ms. Allardyce began the long process of calling out everyone's name and having them stand up. Luckily, she asked everyone to hold their applause which Toby thought might have cut down the time by about five minutes. She looked down at her watch. They'd been in this stuffy meeting a half an hour.

Finally, the headmistress said, "Well, girls, I won't keep you any longer. I'm sure you'll have a perfectly wonderful day, and I look forward to meeting you at some point throughout the day."

"About time," Toby whispered as she got to her feet and stretched out her lanky frame. She felt like she'd been cooped up for hours. She hated these kinds of things. Not the open house, of course, but all the boring meetings people always thought they needed to have before they let you have any fun.

Stepping outside, the girls squinted against the brilliant sunshine and waited for their eyes to adjust from the darkness of the auditorium before they began their walking tour of Canby Hall. It was fun rediscovering the beauty of the campus with the new girls who were completely impressed by what they saw.

They followed the wooded path through the apple orchards that were in full bloom and alive with color. They came out on the edge of the Crowell farm. The white fence served as a border to signal the end of the Canby Hall property.

April climbed up on the fence. "Who lives there?" she asked.

"Friend of mine," Toby said, climbing onto the fence and swinging her leg casually over it to sit on the top rail. "His name is Randy Crowell. I come here to ride horses quite a bit."

"Really?" April asked. "Do you think we could ride this afternoon?"

"I don't think that's such a good idea," Jane said. "P.A. has gone to a lot of trouble to plan all these activities and she might not appreciate our skipping out on them."

"Yeah, I guess you're right," April said, getting down off the fence. "Besides, there'll be all next year to ride horses."

"And don't forget," Andy reminded her, "we signed up for that baseball game this afternoon. It might be kind of obvious if six people didn't show up."

"What are we waiting for?" April asked.

Jane looked at her watch. "Lunch should be ready by the time we get over to the cafeteria."

"That's good," Jennie said.

"You might not think so after you've tried it," Andy said.

"Why?"

"Well, there may be a lot of great things about Canby Hall, but the food isn't one of them."

They came into the cafeteria and much to everyone's surprise, the food actually looked pretty good. There were box lunches on the counter for everyone with club sandwiches and dill pickles and chips inside.

"This looks fairly safe," Jane commented, picking gingerly through the contents of her lunch. "There's not much you can do to a dill pickle and a sealed bag of chips." The other girls laughed.

After lunch they had a sundae party and let everyone make their own ice cream sundaes. The ice cream was pretty soft by the time the girls got around to getting theirs, but it tasted great to everyone.

"I don't know why you're complaining," Jennie said. "You ought to taste the food at Potter High School."

"Well, don't be misled. What you're tasting right now isn't like the food you eat around here every day," Andy said. "It's not usually this good. We wouldn't want to discourage you from coming to school at Canby Hall, but we don't want you to get the wrong idea about the cafeteria. You always keep a good supply of survival food in your room just for self preservation."

"Well," Toby said, pushing her chair back and getting up from the table, "I don't know about anyone else, but I'm ready to play a little baseball."

"I should probably warn you that I'm not too great at baseball," Penny said. "I'm actually a lot better on the bench than I am on the field."

Toby looked over at her and remembered all the other things she supposedly wasn't good at, like horseback riding and dancing and writing. If they were any indication of what she could do on the baseball field, Toby thought cynically, she was probably an all-star player.

They got to the field and the girls decided to pick captains. Maggie and Toby were selected because both girls were good at sports. They began choosing up sides.

Toby took Andy first because she had seen her play and she was a good shortstop. Next she picked April. She took Jennie next and then Jane. She was aware that Maggie was getting some of the better athletes, but she didn't much care. This was just for fun, and Andy would probably get bent out of shape if she let everyone be split up.

She did hesitate, however, before she picked Penny when it came time for her to pick again. She saw Erin Lawson still standing there. Toby knew she was a great outfielder because they'd played on the same team in P.E. Toby paused and then said, "Erin." She felt a jab in the ribs and saw Andy glare coldly at her. "I *know*," Toby whispered. "But we need *some* good players." Toby picked Penny on the next round and eventually they got both teams selected and went to the dugouts on either side of home plate.

Toby offered to be the catcher. Jane suggested they play her in the outfield and April said she didn't care where she played. As it turned out, they would have been better off to have played April in about four positions and moved Jane so far out in the field that she could never touch the ball.

Jane played right field, and it seemed like every hit went directly to her in the first inning. At least she was consistent, Toby thought. She missed them all. The only person out there that looked worse was Penny. Anyway, she had at least been telling the truth when she'd said she couldn't play baseball.

Having both of them in the outfield had been a big mistake. From the looks of it, the only way they'd win this game was if the other team laughed so hard over the comic errors being made, that it couldn't get up to bat.

Toby knew she'd have to alternate playing the two of them. She sat Jane on the bench for the next three innings which Jane didn't seem to mind at all. Toby thought about leaving her there permanently, but the pangs of guilt she experienced forced her to put Jane back in the game. This time she moved her to left field. Almost immediately, all the batters started hitting into left field. Toby figured they were lucky to only be trailing by three runs at the end of the seventh inning.

Jane sat down next to Toby on the bench. "Why do you think all those balls keep coming to me?" she asked, pushing her baseball cap off to one side.

"Because those people up there with the bat keep hitting them. Then you're supposed to *catch* them. That's how you play the game."

"Well, I asked for the outfield because I didn't think anyone would be able to hit it that far. I can't."

"But you don't even look like you're trying to catch the pop ups."

"Well, of course not. You want me to break a nail?" Toby rolled her eyes.

With two outs and Jane at bat, Toby was putting on her catcher's gear when Jane hit a ball and raced down the first base line. The umpire motioned safe as April crossed home plate from third. Jane made it to second base on the overthrow. Toby tore her gear off and hurried up to bat. She decided this was turning out to be some game after all.

She lifted the bat to her shoulder and dared the pitcher to put one across the plate. Jane was showing an unusual amount of enthusiasm yelling to Toby, "Kill it! Kill it!"

Toby watched the ball leave the pitcher's hand. She took careful aim, and slammed one into the hole between the shortstop and second base. While the players scrambled for the ball,

Toby made the most of her hit, sliding into home.

She ran into the dugout and hugged Jane and jumped up and down with the rest of the team. "I was so happy you hit that ball. I didn't expect it. What happened?"

"I kept my eyes open this time," Jane said. All the girls laughed.

Even when the other team won by one run in the last inning, everyone stayed in high spirits. They came off the field laughing and slapping each other on the back anyway. Toby picked up her catcher's gear and started for the locker rooms. Loaded down beneath the gear, she felt something slipping and struggled vainly to keep her hold on the shin guard.

She saw Penny's dark head below her when Penny knelt to pick up the guard. "Here, let me help you." She took the other shin guard and the face mask from Toby and walked with her to the locker room.

"That was some game, huh?" Penny asked.

"Yeah."

"Too bad we lost it."

"Well, it could have been worse." Toby dropped the gear in the corner by the locked cages where they kept the equipment.

"I know the biggest reason we lost is because you picked all of us. You could have had a much better team."

"It doesn't matter. It was just for fun. It

wasn't like this was the World Series or anything," Toby said with a shrug.

"Well, just the same, it was nice of you. You know, that was the first time in my life that I wasn't the last one standing there waiting to get picked?" She smiled self-consciously. "Thanks."

"Sure." Toby bent to organize the catcher's gear and heard Penny's footsteps behind her. She looked up just in time to catch a glimpse of her purple shorts as she went out the door. She ran her fingers through her short red curls. Sometimes she almost thought she could like Penny.

CHAPTER FOURTEEN

Andy opened the door to 407 and stepped aside to allow the other girls to walk by her. Jane and April collapsed onto Jane's bed, which she had made for a change. Andy and Toby had even shamed her into picking up her scattered clothes that morning before everyone arrived. With Jane's things up off the floor, the room actually looked very neat and organized.

Toby flopped onto her bed and Jennie sat on the desk chair next to her. Penny went past Andy and headed for the foot of Andy's bed. Andy closed the door and dropped onto her bed next to Penny.

"I sure never realized baseball was such a tiring sport," Jennie said. "It's a good thing we're only going to the movies tonight. If you had planned anything more strenuous than that, I might have fallen asleep in the middle of it."

"Even ole Jane got into the game there toward the end," Toby said leaning up on her elbows and looking across the room at Jane. "Did you see how excited she got in the seventh inning when it actually looked like we might win?"

"Well, of course I got excited. I finally hit the ball," Jane told them. "I'm just glad I'll have that loud music to keep me from falling asleep tonight."

"What loud music?" April asked.

"Well, Jane won't be coming with us tonight," Andy said somewhat coolly. Even though they had ironed things out earlier, there was still a trace of disapproval in Andy's voice. "Jane's boyfriend's band is playing at a private party tonight."

"Well, I certainly don't blame you for going to hear him instead of going to the movies," Jennie reassured her. "Myself, I love dances."

"Well, I'd really like to invite you all, but it's a private party and there's no way I could do it." Jane felt the redness in her face.

"Hey, speaking of dances," Penny broke in, "did I ever tell you guys about the first big junior high dance I went to?"

Everyone looked over at Penny and Jane felt the tension in the room lessen. She flashed Penny a grateful smile. "I had picked out this terrific knit outfit that my mama insisted was too big on me, but I just knew I looked smashing in it, no matter what my mother said.

"We came home from the store and I decided to model the outfit for my older brothers who were home from school at the time. My mother had these high heels that matched the dress perfectly, and I talked her into letting me borrow them. They were a little big, and I'd stuffed tissue in the toes to make them fit better.

"I came wobbling into the room like a leaf in a wind storm, and both of my brothers started laughing. They said I'd be lucky to walk, let alone dance. Being the stubborn kid that I am, that made me even more determined to wear that outfit that I knew made me look older and more mature.

"I didn't pay any attention to what they said and the night of the dance I got all dressed up in that outfit and my mother's too-big shoes and staggered into the library where my father told me I looked beautiful and my mother tried to hide her smile behind her hand. Feeling like a beauty queen, I swept regally from the room and went out to the car."

By now, Penny was up on her feet and pantomiming the walk to the car, her ankles caving in to the middle. Everyone was laughing, including Penny.

"I got to the dance and my feet were killing me, not to mention my ankles. It felt like I'd been on ice skates for days. I made my way to a chair and politely turned down all the boys who asked me to dance. Then Scotty Turner came over and asked me to dance and I just about died. I thought Scotty Turner was the cutest boy in the whole world and I'd been in love with him since second grade.

"So I figured, why not? It's just one little dance. When he slid the chair back, my knit skirt got caught under the leg of it and when I stood up, my skirt didn't come with me. I stepped right out of it and left it laying on the floor crumpled under the leg of the chair.

"Scotty hadn't noticed anything was wrong yet. I looked down and saw nothing but my slip and knew I had a big decision to make. Should I go out there and hope everyone thought it was my skirt or should I grab my skirt and head to the bathroom in a hurry?

"Well, I looked into his gorgeous brown eyes and decided it was worth the gamble. I hoped if I kept his eyes locked on mine he wouldn't look down and he might not notice anything out of the ordinary. We moved out onto the floor and began dancing and this creepy little girl named Margaret Fletcher came up to me and said, 'Excuse me, Penelope, but it looks like you're not wearing a skirt.'

"Scotty looked down and his face got bright red. I looked down too and said, 'Oh my gosh, when did that happen?' and quickly grabbed the skirt from underneath the chair and ran into the bathroom to get dressed. I had long since kicked off my mother's shoes and I made good time going into the bathroom. I pulled on my skirt, tried to fluff up my hair with my fingers because my purse was still out on the table, and I went out to find Scotty and my shoes."

Penny moved over and leaned against the desk. "Ms. Anderlik, the advisor, came up to me and quietly whispered, 'Dear, your slip is showing.' I started to laugh and said, 'So what?'

"I never did find one of my mother's shoes, but I finally located Scotty. He was dancing with Margaret. I gave up and went home early promising myself I would never dance again.

"I gave the outfit to my mother to make up for the shoe I'd lost, and I avoided Scotty Turner like the plague." Everyone laughed and it crossed Toby's mind that maybe not everything Penny said was the truth, but it certainly was entertaining.

"I can see where that might make you a little hesitant to go to dances," Andy laughed.

There was a knock at the door. "What's going on in here?" Dee asked. "You guys sure are making a lot of noise."

"Sorry," Andy said still smiling.

"No, that's okay. I just came by to say hi."

"Excuse me," Jane said suddenly, getting up from the bed. "I'll be right back."

As she went downstairs to the phone booths, she couldn't help smiling when she thought about Penny. Closing the phone booth door, she dialed Cary's number.

"Hello," she said. "It's me."

"Jane, hey!" Cary's familiar voice came over the other end of the receiver.

"Hi," she said. She wondered what *had* prompted her to call. She was shocked to find that she was hoping in a way he might actually break their date. That would free her to go out with everyone tonight without having to make a choice between Cary and her friends.

"It's a good thing you called. I'll be a few minutes late. Don't give up on me though."

"No, I won't."

"Hey, is something wrong? You sound down."

"No, everything's fine. I'm just a little tired. We played this baseball game today and then we've been sitting around listening to Penny's great adventures at her first big dance."

"Gee, that does sound exhausting," he teased.

"Oh, never mind. I'll see you tonight."

"Can't wait," he said.

"Me neither," Jane answered. But she wasn't nearly as excited at the thought of going out tonight as she was two days ago. She really must be tired, she thought.

She came back to 407 and stood outside the door listening to the laughter from inside the room. The whole day had been crazy and fun and she actually felt a little jealous that she was going to have to miss the rest of the evening.

Then she wondered what she was thinking. She was with these girls all the time, it was no big deal if she missed a night. Cary, on the other hand, was offering her a chance to do something really special and memorable, and here she was acting like he was dragging her off to the dentist or something. She put a smile on her face and pushed the door open.

"Where did you go, or do I need to ask?" April said. "From that smile, I'll bet it's something to do with the guy with the band."

"And you'll be right," Jane said.

"Must be something pretty special to get you that happy," Jennie said.

"Must be something pretty special to get her to desert all of us tonight," Andy said. A quick heated look flashed between the two of them and then it was gone. Andy got up from the bed and said, "Well, the rest of us better get around or we'll hit Pizza Pete's just about the time the rush gets there."

"I'm going to go on down to my room and get cleaned up," Penny said. "One of you can come with me if you want," she offered, "but I better warn you, there're still boxes around the room."

April got up. "I'll go with you."

"Okay. We'll be back here in thirty minutes," Penny said. Andy could hear her voice as they went down the hall. "See, I was in the middle of unpacking when it struck me that the school year was almost over and if I unpacked all this stuff, I'd just have to pack it all up again in no time, so I'm saving myself the trouble. . . ." Her voice trailed off down the hall.

"I'm going down to the showers," Andy said getting a towel from the closet.

"I'll come with you," Toby said.

"Got an extra towel?" Jennie asked.

"Sure, come on. What's a trip to Canby Hall without seeing the shower room?" The three of them went out leaving Jane in the silence of the empty room. It was hard to believe just a few minutes ago, it had been alive with the sounds of talking and laughter and now it seemed deserted and lonely. She picked up her hair brush and went over to the mirror and began brushing her long, thick hair. She noticed that her reflection, staring back at her, didn't look very happy for a girl who was about to spend the evening of her life at the Westfield.

Chapter Fifteen

Jane stood at the mirror deep in thought until the laughter echoing down the hall brought her face back into focus for her. The door slammed open, banging loudly against the wall, and Toby rushed through.

"I won."

"Not fair," Jennie laughed breathlessly. "You had a head start. I was still picking up my towel when you took off."

"Hey," Toby said shooting her wadded up towel toward the clothes basket, "around here you gotta be fast."

"Yeah, or sneaky," Jennie answered back tossing her own towel into the basket on top of Toby's.

Andy came in and closed the door behind her. "I don't know why you two bothered to take a shower if you're only going to work up a sweat again."

She sat at her desk and began picking out

her curly black hair. Jennie took a small mirror and a tube of lip gloss from her purse and went over near the window to catch the late afternoon sun while she applied it.

"Here," Jane said stepping aside. "You can use this mirror. I'm not leaving for a while yet. Cary's going to be a little late."

"Thanks." She moved over next to Jane. Jane studied Jennie's short brown hair. Streaks of lighter strands that were almost blonde ran through it, appearing to be the sun's natural frost. Her skin was clear and smooth, and free of make-up. She looked the perfect type girl for Canby Hall. Then Jane decided that was a silly thing to think. Looking at her vastly different roommates Jane decided there really was no one type of girl at Canby Hall. That was what made it so fun.

Jennie turned away from the mirror. "Thanks," she said. She saw that Andy had slipped into her yellow walking shorts and a brightly-colored, cotton-knit sweater, and clipped a yellow bow into her curly dark hair.

"You look cute," Jennie said. Jane looked over and smiled. "She always does."

"Thanks," Andy replied. She leaned over and tied her other white tennis shoe.

"Hey, what about me?" Toby asked. She had finally shed the jeans she seemed to be in constantly and was wearing a pair of khaki shorts and a red short-sleeved knit polo shirt.

"My gosh." Andy clutched her chest and

fell back against the wall. "I didn't know you had anything but jeans."

"See? You learn something new every day." She went past the other girls. "You ready?"

"Yeah," Andy said. "Just let me grab my wallet. Why don't you guys go on down to Penny's and tell her we'll meet her in the lobby?"

"Okay," Jennie said as she followed Toby out the door.

Jane sat down at her desk and watched Andy search for her wallet. "It's on the chest of drawers," she told her.

"Thanks." Andy went over and stuffed the wallet in her pocket. She stopped at the mirror and gave herself one last look. For a split second, Jane thought about going with her.

"Hey," Jane said. Andy stopped in the doorway and looked back. "Have a good time." Andy nodded and then she was gone.

Jane went to the closet and stood in front of the open door deciding what she was going to wear. She pulled out several outfits and held them up in front of the mirror. She didn't like any of them. She needed Toby or Andy to tell her what looked good. She finally decided on a simple black dress with small rhinestone buttons.

She pulled on her black hose and put the dress on and went to the mirror. She felt like she was going to a funeral instead of a party. She dabbed at her long lashes with mascara and blinked at her reflection in the mirror. She sucked in her cheeks and took blush from her makeup bag before making upward strokes at either side of her face. Next, she pulled the sides of her hair back and turned her head from side to side. Finally, she took even clumps of hair from either side of her head and pulled it up into pigtails and stuck her tongue out at herself.

"Jane Barrett, you are acting like a dope," she scolded herself. "Here you are about to spend the most memorable evening of your life at the classy Westfield Hotel and you would rather be getting indigestion at Pizza Pete's."

She went over to her desk and sat down. It would have been so great if everything hadn't come up on this particular weekend. But they'd been planning open house for weeks and she felt guilty for deserting everyone tonight.

But there was something else, too. It wasn't just the fun she'd had that day, or the fact that her friends would go right on having fun that night without her. She had made plans with her friends, and no real friend would cancel plans as she had just because a boy asked her out.

Jane pictured herself sitting at some corner table near the band waiting for Cary to finish his set so he could spend a few minutes with her before he went back to play again. It wouldn't really make much difference if she was there or not. Why had the whole thing sounded like so much fun the other night?

Suddenly, Jane knew what she wanted to do. She began pulling clothes from her drawers looking for her white shorts. She found them neatly folded and lying beneath some T-shirts. She grabbed them and went to the closet to look for a shirt to wear with them. Her red and white striped polo was hanging right in front of her. She pulled it from the hanger and tossed it onto the bed along with her shorts. She stepped out of her shoes as she began unzipping her dress. If she hurried, she would still be able to get to Pizza Pete's before they left.

Jane was standing in front of the mirror tying the last red ribbon around her pigtail, when her buzzer sounded signaling her that she had a guest in the lobby. She stepped into her sandals and ran downstairs to meet him.

Cary's mouth dropped open at the sight of her. *"You're* going to the Westfield dressed like that?"

"Well, that's what I wanted to talk to you about," Jane said hesitantly. "I'm not going to the Westfield at all."

"You're not what?" Cary took her arm and guided her through the lobby and out onto the front porch. "Now, would you like to tell me what's going on?"

"I don't know if I *can* explain it exactly, but

we've been planning open house for weeks and at first I didn't think it would matter to anyone if I wasn't there tonight. But it did matter, especially to me. I really *do* want to go with you. And if it was any other night but this one, I would."

"I don't get it. What's so great about having a pizza and seeing a movie? You can do that anytime. I'm offering you a night at the Westfield and you're passing it up to spend the evening in Greenleaf?" He ran his hand through his hair and shook his head in disbelief. "This makes no sense at all, Jane."

"To me it does. If I don't see the Westfield tonight, there'll be other chances. It'll always be there. But tonight is one that I promised to spend with Toby and Andy and the other girls."

"Well, that's real good, Jane. But we had a date for tonight. How come *that's* not important to you?" He turned around and jumped off the porch and almost ran to his car.

Jane stood and watched him go thinking she should stop him, but knowing she wasn't going to. He'd come around; and if he didn't, she still knew she'd made the right decision.

She rushed down the steps and across the campus toward Greenleaf. The flashing neon sign in front of Pizza Pete's caused her to quicken her step and hope she wasn't too late to catch them before they'd left. Jane pushed the door open. It was noisy and crowded. She stood in the doorway looking from table to table trying to spot Andy or Toby. Finally she saw them in a little booth near the back.

She dodged her way through the tables and chairs and came up behind Andy. She leaned on the back of her chair and looked at the few remaining pieces of pizza on the large silver tray in the center of the table.

"Well, did you guys save me a piece?"

Andy spun around on the chair and everyone else looked over in surprise. "Jane what are you doing here?" Andy asked.

"You're supposed to be having dinner at the Westfield," Toby reminded her.

"What's dinner at the Westfield when you can have pizza with your friends?" She nudged Penny and said, "Move over, I'm starving."

CHAPTER SIXTEEN

Sunday morning, Patrice Allardyce looked out among the girls seated in the small chapel of Canby Hall and smiled warmly. "Girls, you've made this a lovely weekend with all your hard work. All the brochures and cumulative averages in the world can't sell this school as well as each of you. I'd like to show my appreciation with a small open house this afternoon. I encourage you to stop by between 2:00 and 4:00."

Andy and Jane exchanged looks before catching a glimpse of the scowl on Toby's face. "What's wrong?" Andy whispered.

"I was hoping to get out to Randy's this afternoon. Maybe we can make an early appearance and be done with it."

"Now who's deserting us?" Jane teased.

The services ended and the three roommates walked back to Baker House. Coming down the hall toward their room, they passed

Penny's room. She was sitting in the middle of the unmade bed holding her writing table on her lap. Boxes were pretty much as they had been since she'd moved in with the exception that now they were pushed off to one side.

"Missed you at chapel," Andy said pushing the door open and stepping into the room.

Penny looked up from her writing. "Oh, hi."

"We're going to an open house at P.A.'s this afternoon. Thought you'd like to come along and be our guide."

"Sorry, I can't. I still have some work to do on this essay."

"You mean you haven't finished that yet?" Jane asked.

"No," Penny said looking over at her with wide eyes. "Have you?"

"I was going to work on it tonight."

"It was a lot easier before Ms. Gardner decided she liked my writing. I didn't care what I wrote before, but now I feel like she expects something from me and it makes me nervous, I guess."

"That's the way it is with you writers. You're creative," Andy said as she stepped over near the bed to see what Penny was writing. Her foot got tangled up in a damp towel. "And you're both messy."

"But you know what I like the most about

you?" Jane said looking contentedly around her.

"What's that?"

"You're about the only person I know who makes me look neat." Jane laughed and Penny did too.

"Now I wouldn't go that far," Andy began.

"Look, you guys, I hate to miss this rousing debate as to who wins the Best Mess Award, but I've got this great idea that if I get over to Randy's now, I can catch a ride on Maxine and still get back here by 2:30. That would put us at P.A.'s by 3:00. How's that?"

"An hour of P.A. is about all anybody needs," Andy agreed.

"Later, then." Toby dashed off to the room. She pulled a pair of jeans from the drawer and shook them out. She drew them over her slim legs, then pulled on a cotton T-shirt, and her favorite boots.

She took the stairs two at a time headed down to the lobby. Running across campus, she could almost feel the warm wind whipping through her hair as she imagined herself on the back of Maxine. She came through the trees and out into the clearing that backed up to Randy's place. Maxine was standing in the corral and whinnied when she saw Toby running toward her.

"Hey, stranger," Randy yelled from inside the barn. "How was the big open house?"

"Great. It was lots of fun."

"Too bad I missed it," he said coming out of the barn.

"They wouldn't have let you come anyway. Somehow, I don't think you could ever pass for a Canby Hall girl." Randy came over and put his arm around her and walked back into the barn with her to get Maxine's saddle.

"Got time for a quick ride with me?" Toby asked.

"That's what I'm here for." He pulled his own saddle from the boards of the stall and began saddling his horse while she went out and put the saddle on Maxine. Toby talked softly to her as she worked at the cinch and bridle.

Randy came out of the barn on his horse. "Ready?"

She grabbed hold of the saddle horn and hoisted herself easily onto the saddle. Neither of them spoke as they rode along the dusty road of the Crowell farm. Toby thought of Texas springs and her own horse Max. It was hard to believe that in just a few weeks she would be back there riding him again. She gently nudged Maxine in the side and the horse took off. It was exhilarating to feel the wind and the hot sun. She felt like she could ride all the way back to Texas.

They got back to the corral and Toby hopped off Maxine and pulled the saddle from her sweaty back. She carried the heavy saddle into the barn and took the curry comb and brush from the shelf. She stopped and got a pail of oats for Maxine and went out to find Randy standing next to his horse and gazing off toward Canby Hall.

"She's gonna miss you this summer," he said.

"Well, I'm not going anywhere for a while."

"Couple more weeks and she'll be back to hauling me around for exercise."

"Yeah, well, I'll be back in the fall." Toby rubbed her shiny coat with long even strokes and the horse moved her head in gentle contentment.

"She's not the only one who's going to miss you, you know." Toby looked over at Randy who was still staring off into space.

"Oh, yeah?"

"It's not easy to find someone who's so comfortable to be with that you don't even need words. That's the way it is with us. And I'm going to miss seeing you around here."

"Well, I'll miss you guys, too," she said, patting the horse's neck. She looked around at the white farm house and the green landscape that looked like a picture postcard. "I never thought when I first got here that I'd ever get used to it, let alone miss it, but I will."

"Hey, listen to us. We sound like you're

leaving in the morning and never coming back." He laughed and rubbed her head affectionately.

"Well, you've got me around for two more years." She took Maxine's reins and led her to her stall. She glanced at Randy's watch and saw it was 2:10. "Is your watch right?"

"You bet. Takes a licking and keeps on ticking."

"I'm supposed to be ready to go to an open house in twenty minutes. I've got to run."

"See you later," he called as she ran out of the barn and hopped up over the fence. She waved one hand in the air and disappeared into the orchard.

Jane and Andy were dressed and waiting for her when she burst into the room, hot and sweaty. "I just have to take a quick shower," she said apologetically. "I'll be ready in ten minutes."

She dashed down the hall pulling her clothes off as she went. She jumped into the shower and felt the cool spray wash off the sweat and dirt of the afternoon. Toby grabbed a towel and patted herself dry and rushed back to the room. She went over to the closet and stared at the clothes hanging there.

"I suppose jeans are out, huh?"

"Definitely," Jane answered. She got up from her desk and took a light blue skirt from the closet and hung it in front of Toby. "Try this."

"I can't believe it. The most beautiful Sunday afternoon we've had all year and I'm spending it in a skirt!"

When the girls got to Patrice Allardyce's, they were shown through the house and out onto the patio where everyone was gathered around a table filled with delicious cookies and cakes. Toby filled her plate, then began putting things on Jane and Andy's plates.

"I'll never eat all that," Jane protested.

"Yes, but I will, and if I have to wear this stupid skirt, there has to be some fun in it." She smiled wickedly at Jane and popped a cookie into her mouth.

Ms. Allardyce tapped a knife against the crystal punch bowl and said, "May I have your attention, please? Girls, could I have your attention?"

The noise began to subside and the girls all stopped what they were doing and turned toward her. "I know this is a festive occasion and I promise not to make any long speeches, but I just wanted to tell you again how pleased I am that open house was such a success.

"Canby Hall isn't these buildings, or the instructors, or myself, or the board of directors. It's you. And that's why the open house was a success. When you leave here, you'll take a lot more than an education with you. You'll take memories that will last a lifetime. Friends that you can always count on no matter how many years you're away from them. Canby Hall isn't a school. It's a feeling we all share. I'm sure that Julia Canby would be very happy about that if she knew. And so am I. Enjoy your tea, girls."

Patrice Allardyce went back into the house amid the applause of the girls gathered on the lawn. Jane reached out and took hold of Andy and Toby. Who would have ever thought looking at that unlikely trio that they would become best friends? But they were the best friends Jane had ever known. She thought she could write that essay on friendship now, because she finally knew what it was all about.

Sitting at her desk deep in thought, Jane didn't even hear the knock at the door. She jumped when she heard Maggie's voice saying, "Hey, Jane, you've got a visitor."

Jane got up and went toward the door. She caught a glimpse of her reflection in the mirror. Her hair looked a mess from running her hands through it while she had been trying to concentrate. She nearly picked up her brush to fix it, then settled for fluffing it up with her hands. She had no idea who was in the lobby, but they would have to take her like she was.

Coming down the stairs, Jane didn't see anyone at first. She stopped toward the bottom step and looked around. She went over to the desk to ask Meredith if she knew anything about a guest. She would shoot Maggie if she'd been fooling around. Jane had been on a roll with her essay and now it would take her awhile to get back into writing it.

Meredith was reading a book when Jane came up to the desk. "Excuse me," Jane said softly.

Meredith looked up. Her stylish camel-colored frames slid down her dainty nose and she pushed them back onto her face. "Oh, hi, Jane."

"Maggie said there was someone waiting for me down here."

"Yes, there is."

Jane looked around the lobby in confusion. "Well, they're awfully small or I need to borrow your glasses."

Meredith laughed. "No, he's waiting on the porch." She nodded her head in that general direction and went back to her book. Jane looked out through the glass. She saw the back of Cary's head. She noticed his long hair gently moving in the soft breeze and wanted to touch it. Then she wished she had taken the time to brush her own hair. She didn't know what he wanted, but she knew she wanted to look her best.

Jane fluffed her hair again and took a deep breath. "Thanks," she said and went out the front doors. "Hi," she said softly.

He turned abruptly and she almost caught her breath at how good-looking he was. The late afternoon sun caught him just right and seemed to set his face aglow. "Hi," he said.

"How was the dance last night?"

"Fine. How was the movie?"

"Fine."

He shifted his weight uneasily and pushed his hands into the pockets of his baggies. "Hey, you want to take a walk?"

"Sure."

They went down the steps, neither of them saying anything for a while. "I thought about what you said last night," Cary finally said. "And I guess maybe I can understand a little why you backed out on me."

"I'm glad."

"I mean, at first, I was really ticked. Then I got to thinking what I'd do if one of the guys just didn't show up to play last night because something else came up and I could sort of see your point."

"I guess what it comes down to is not letting your friends down."

"Yeah, well, I'd like to think I'm your friend too."

"You are," Jane assured him. She reached over and took his chin in her hand and pulled his head down so she could look into his blue eyes. "I hope I didn't let you down too much last night."

"In a way you did, but I'll get over it." Jane let a smile spread across her face. "This time," he added, "but next time it'd be a lot easier on everyone if you knew what you wanted up front and you were honest about it."

"Believe me, I learned my lesson. I'm not putting myself in that position again."

"Good." Cary let himself show affection for the first time since he'd arrived and put his hand in hers. "Now that we got that settled, I seem to remember promising you a dinner. But I'm afraid you'll have to settle for a pizza in Greenleaf instead of a steak at the Westfield."

"Know what?" Jane gave his hand a playful squeeze. "I bet it'll taste just as good."

Monday afternoon's English class was listless. The girls, still tired from the full weekend, had dragged themselves through the day and had finally gotten to the end. Ms. Gardner didn't help matters when she gave them a reading assignment. Many of the girls had their heads propped on their hands and were fighting to stay awake.

Toby was actually enjoying the story for a change. It was a thing called "The Quiet Man" and she remembered seeing the movie on television a long time ago. John Wayne had starred in it and as she read, she imagined him and all the other characters vividly.

About ten minutes before class was over, Ms. Gardner pushed her chair back and came around to the front of her desk. "Girls, I have taken the opportunity to glance over the papers you handed in earlier, and I am quite pleased with what I'm seeing."

She reached behind her and took one of the essays from her desk. "Before we leave today, I'd like to read one of these to you that I feel is particularly well written." Ms. Gardner leaned back against the edge of her desk and began to read.

"Friendship seems like an easy thing to write about. Everybody has friends. But I learned an important lesson about friendship this weekend. There is nothing easy about it; whether it's writing about friendships or forming them. Building a friendship is hard work and relationships will wither and die if both people don't work constantly at keeping them alive."

Toby leaned back in her seat and looked longingly out the window. She really couldn't understand why Ms. Gardner got such a kick out of reading these stupid essays to the whole class. She could understand if the woman liked to read them to herself, after all, she assigned them, she must like to read them.

But why make the whole class suffer through it with her?

Toby turned her attention to the front of the room again and heard Ms. Gardner reading: "When I think back to when I returned to Canby Hall this year, I can't help but remember the first impression I had of my two roommates and my wondering if I would ever be able to live with these girls I had so little in common with. But in spite of those differences we became friends; and because of them, we've been able to stay friends."

Toby sighed loudly and several girls sitting around her stared in her direction. She was able to catch Andy's attention and was given a warning glance from Andy telling her to settle down. Toby nodded her head and rolled her eyes toward the ceiling before getting out her pencil and beginning one of her favorite pastimes, writing her own captions under the pictures in her English Lit book.

Toby wrote what she felt was a particularly witty caption and giggled softly to herself. She looked around for someone to share it with. She noticed Andy was still entranced by what Ms. Gardner was saying and when she looked over at Jane, she noticed Jane had her hands entwined on her desk top and was studying them intensely, not looking at anyone around her. Toby thought maybe she should listen and see what was going on.

"After hours of planning for open house, something else came up at the last minute," Ms. Gardner read. "I nearly deserted my friends because that something else sounded like it might be more fun at the time." Then Toby realized the essay she was supposed to be listening to was Jane's. She set her pen down and started paying attention.

"I was angry with them for not understanding and certain that if they got the chance they would react the same way. But I think now that they probably wouldn't have changed their plans, because they knew something I had to find out for myself. The best memories you may ever have probably won't be made at a private party at the Westfield Inn, but rather sharing a pizza with your friends in Greenleaf. And when I think about Canby Hall, I probably won't remember the times I spent with some boy that I might have long since stopped dating, but long talks I had with my roommates and best friends in Room 407."

Ms. Gardner set the essay on the desk behind her and stood up. "I realize there's still five minutes till the bell, but I can't think of a better way to end the class, so why don't we slip out quietly and enjoy the rest of this beautiful day?"

The lifeless expressions on the girl's faces broke into smiles as they began gathering books and getting out of their desks before Ms. Gardner had a chance to reconsider.

Andrea caught up with Jane in the doorway. "That was some essay."

"Yeah, well. . . ." Jane's face flushed with color. "When I wrote it, I didn't expect her to read it to the whole class. I hope it didn't embarrass you."

"Why would I be embarrassed by it? I thought it was terrific. How many people have their friendship immortalized in sophomore English?"

Chapter Seventeen

A couple of days later Jane nearly ran over two girls who were trying to make their way to the mailboxes. She clutched the letter from the *Canby Hall Journal* in her hand afraid to open it until she reached the privacy of her room. What if they had rejected her story? She couldn't let herself think about it. It was too important to her.

She closed the door and leaned against it. She held the letter to her chest for a minute before she opened it. She looked at the envelope once more before she put her finger beneath the flap and gently slid it open. She lifted the sheet from inside and read the first line.

"Thank you for your submission to the *Canby Hall Journal*. We are pleased to accept it as one of the twelve features in this year's magazine. . . ."

She didn't need to read any further. They

had taken her story! She let out an uncharacteristic whoop of excitement and ran out of the room in search of somebody she knew. It could be anybody at all. She wanted to tell everyone. She was going to be published. Her first story would be in print in less than a month.

Toby was coming up the stairs reading a rare letter from home when Jane grabbed her and almost knocked her off her feet. "Hey, what's going on here? You nearly knocked me down the stairs."

"The best thing just happened. My story got accepted for the *Journal.*" Jane waved the letter in front of Toby's face.

Toby wrinkled her brow in confusion. "What *Journal*?"

"Honestly, Tobe, the *Canby Hall Journal.* I've only worked on it for about three weeks."

"Well, hey, that's great." Toby began walking toward the room.

"This is it. I'm on my way now. Well, I mean, I still have a lot of work ahead of me. But, I'm published! Oh, Toby, do you know what this means?" Jane squeezed Toby in an excited embrace.

"No. But I do know you're breaking my ribs."

"Oh, sorry." Just then Jane spotted Dee and Maggie coming up the hall. "Hey, you guys, guess what?"

Toby watched her fly down the hall before

turning into their room. Well, she lived with a writer and a dancer. Maybe they'd both be famous one day. "What you going to do with your life, Houston?" she asked herself as she lay down on her bed.

Probably raise horses on my dad's ranch and be happier than anyone, she thought. She saw herself tearing across the flat Texas terrain on Max chasing wild horses. There would be other riders following her, but no one would be able to catch the two of them.

The knock at the door brought her out of her reverie. She sat up and said, "Yeah?"

Penny pushed the door open timidly. "Is Andy here?"

Toby looked around the room in mock seriousness. "Nope. I don't see her."

"Well, do you know anything about this?" She was holding a letter that looked a lot like the one Jane had just shown her.

"Is that Jane's acceptance to the journal?"

"No. It's mine, I guess."

"No kidding? Looks like everyone's a writer these days."

"But I didn't mean to be. I mean, I. . . ."

Andrea stepped into the doorway behind Penny. "What's up?"

"Maybe you can tell me," Penny said. "Do you know anything about this?" She held the letter out to Andy who took it and read it. Andy broke into a wide grin.

"They took it, huh? I just *knew* it was good enough. That's terrific."

"Just what exactly did they take?" Penny asked in dismay.

"The story you wrote about the Disney vacation."

"But you had no right!" Penny cried indignantly.

"Well, you did give it to me. You said I could do whatever I wanted with it," Andrea defended herself, "and that's what I wanted to do with it."

"But I gave it to *you*," Penny said with a mixture of anger and hurt. "You knew I didn't want it submitted to that stupid magazine and you did it anyway. I just can't believe you'd do something like this." Penny shook the crumpled letter in Andy's face.

"Well, since I did and they want the story, why not just be happy about it?" Andy said, still convinced that she had done the right thing.

"Happy about it? You can't be serious. They want to see me. They want to talk about a few changes."

"So?"

"So! I don't know how to make changes. What if I can't write the story they want? Then what? I thought you were my friend. How could you do this to me?"

"I am your friend. I was trying to help."

"Well, if you want to help, go over there and get my story back."

"I can't do that."

"Well, I can."

"I guess you'll have to tell them I made a mistake." Andy's voice betrayed the disappointment she felt.

"You sure did," Toby said. Andy and Penny looked toward her in surprise. Both girls had forgotten Toby was even in the room. "You made the mistake of thinking that Penny wanted to be something besides cute. And you know what?" Toby said walking over to Penny. "You're going to play that role so long that if you *do* decide you want to do something else, you won't know how."

"I don't know what you're talking about," Penny said as tears began to slide down her cheeks.

"Oh, yeah? Well, let's start off with the riding lesson you didn't really need. Anybody that's been around horses would have known that you knew exactly what you were doing that day. You know how to ride, don't you? But when Randy offered to take you riding, instead of getting on that horse and taking off, you had to give him that helpless act you're so good at. Maybe it's time you figured out, there's a lot of things you can be in life besides 'cute'."

Penny stared at Toby with a tear-streaked face for an instant. Then she turned and bolted from the room, nearly knocking Jane down on her way out.

"What was that all about?" Jane asked. Then she saw the letter in Andrea's hand. "Oh. It got rejected, huh?" she asked sympathetically.

"Just the opposite." Andy held the letter out to Jane. "I don't get it. I thought this would prove something to her. I wanted to show her she can be something in addition to being somebody's wife and mother if she wants to be," Andy said.

"Well, obviously she doesn't want to be," Toby said. Andrea sat down on her bed and opened the crumpled letter Penny had left behind. It began much the same as Jane's. It was very complimentary of her writing style and content. But the second paragraph asked for some minor revision on the end of the story that the editors felt would make the story more believable to the readers.

Well, Andy had done all she could. She'd submitted the story for her, but she couldn't very well do the revision. That was something Penny would have to do herself. Andy still believed that she made the right choice in submitting the story, and she didn't want to give up so easily when she was so close to convincing Penny she could stand on her own.

"I'm going down to talk to Penny. You want to come?" Andy looked from Toby to Jane.

"I've already said all I need to say," Toby answered.

"How about you?" Andy asked turning to Jane.

"I'm not so sure I do. Penny knows what she wants."

"I don't think she does. I think she wants to change, but she's afraid. I could really use your help." Andrea stood in the doorway and looked hopefully at Jane.

"I think this is something you need to do on your own," Jane said. "It's between you and Penny."

"Maybe you're right," Andy said. She pressed the wrinkled page flat with her hand. "Wish me luck," she said, waving the paper at them as she left.

Penny's door was partially shut and it glided open when Andy knocked. "Yeah?" Penny said looking up from the middle of her rumpled bed where she sat hugging a giant teddy bear. The wadded Kleenex and her red rimmed eyes made it obvious that she had been crying.

"You left this in my room." Andy extended her hand with the letter toward Penny. Penny stared at the letter, but made no effort to take it. Andy sat it on the bed next to her.

"I'm sorry. I didn't mean to cause you any trouble. I thought it would be just the push you needed to build your confidence."

"I don't know what to do," Penny said

miserably. "I'm scared. They want me to make changes. What if I can't do it? Or if, when I get done, they still don't like it? Then what?"

"Then you say, 'What do they know? It's just a little school magazine.' Right?" Andy sat down on the bed next to her.

"But don't you see? I always wanted to write, but I was afraid that I wouldn't be good enough."

"Here's your chance to find out," Andy said patting Penny's leg encouragingly.

"I'm not so sure I want to find out."

"What you're saying is you'd rather keep your dreams tucked away some place than take a chance on trying to make them come true?" Penny nodded. "It might be a lot safer, but it sure will be boring."

Andy got up from the bed and looked back at Penny. "I guess maybe you do need someone to take care of you if that's the way you feel about it." She walked out and left Penny sitting in the middle of her unmade bed.

Penny tossed and turned all night. She would doze off only to wake up again and glance over at the clock near her bed and see it was fifteen minutes later than it had been the last time she'd checked.

Things that Andy and Toby had said to her kept dancing around in her head. There were so many thoughts and worries on her mind that she wanted to just pack everything up and tell her parents to come get her right now.

She thought she knew what she wanted: to find some nice boy, get married, and be a good wife. Then she met all these girls who had plans to be that and something more. And she started wondering if she wanted something more as well.

Penny sat up and leaned back against the headboard of her bed. She hugged her knees and thought about what she was going to do in the morning. If she took the story back, that would be the end of it. But even if she tore it into a hundred pieces, things would be different now. Andy would be disappointed in her.

And no matter how she tried, she couldn't get Toby's voice out of her head. She heard Toby accusing her of not wanting to succeed. Putting on a helpless act for everybody. Penny had never really thought about it like that before, but she had been pretending for years. It got her out of a lot of things she didn't want to do while she was growing up. Now it looked like she was going to have to decide if she should stop pretending and grow up.

After her last morning class, Penny stood outside the journalism room and tried to calm her frantic nerves. She had barely been able to concentrate on anything all morning. She was going to have to get this over with now or she would lose her nerve.

Penny still wasn't sure *what* she was going to do. Would she walk in there and collect her essay and let things continue like they'd gone for the last fifteen years? Or would she talk to that editor about the changes and take a gamble at pleasing herself for a change? Penny opened the door to the journalism room still uncertain about what she wanted.

She stepped into the chaos around her. The busy students never even looked up from the clacking typewriters. She glanced around, looking for what she hoped would be the editor. Behind a glass partition sat the journalism teacher with a pencil jutting out from behind her ear. She thoughtfully studied the papers in front of her. She must be the editor, too, Penny thought.

Timidly, Penny tapped softly on the glass. The lady appeared not to hear her. Penny knocked a little harder and said, "Excuse me."

The woman looked up sharply at being interrupted. Then her face softened. "Yes?"

"I'm Penny Vanderark . . ." Penny began.

"Penny Vanderark?" the woman repeated, sounding like she didn't have a clue as to who Penny Vanderark was.

"I'm here about my story for the *Canby Hall Journal*," Penny prompted.

"Oh," she said, setting her glasses on the

desk. "Yes. Of course. Now I remember." She got up and went to a bin on top of a file cabinet behind her. She opened a folder and shuffled through the papers and pulled out her manuscript. "Here it is."

She came back over to the desk and slid her glasses onto her face. "Now there are just a couple changes I'd like to see here," she said as she skimmed over the paper.

Penny stood nervously at her side, trying to work up the nerve to ask her what she wanted done. But that might lead this lady to think that Penny was interested in doing it, and Penny wasn't sure that was what she wanted yet.

"Aw, yes, here it is." She set the story on the desk in front of her. "Now, here at the end, I'd like to see you expand on this section. It's a very funny part, but it's too brief. Beef it up."

Penny reread what she'd written and was pleased with what she found. As the editor continued, Penny was even more surprised to find herself disagreeing with what she was saying. Then the shock of the realization hit her that she *did* like the story, and the changes this woman wanted wouldn't make it her story anymore.

Feeling her stomach tie itself into a tight ball, Penny reached one small shaking hand out and took the paper from the desk. She read it again to be sure she was right and then she said, "I'm sorry if you can't use my story in the *Journal*, but I like the ending and that's the way I want it to stay."

Penny took her paper and turned to leave the glassed-in office. She had come here not knowing what to do. Worrying about how to ask for her paper back or worrying about her ability to make the revisions, if she decided to leave the story in the *Journal*. But never once did she dream that she would not let her story be printed because she disagreed with the changes they wanted her to make. She had made a decision about something she believed in, and right or wrong, she'd done it all by herself.

"Ms. Vanderark." Penny turned around almost expecting to see her mother. No one ever called her anything but Penny. The journalism teacher was making her way through the crowded tables toward her. "Tell you what, why don't you leave this story with me and let me take another look at it? It's a good story and I really think it belongs in the *Journal*."

Penny held the story out to her and noticed her hand wasn't shaking anymore. This was turning out to be some morning. She had become a writer and her own person all at once. She could hardly wait to tell Andy.

Toby, Andy, and Jane were coming across the campus heading toward the cafeteria for lunch when Penny came running up to them. She was flushed and excited. "Andy, guess what? I'm not going to do it. The revision, I mean."

"I knew that yesterday." Andy continued walking.

"But don't you want to know why?" While the three girls kept walking toward Baker House, Penny was walking backward and fairly bouncing with excitement.

"I give up. Why?"

"Because it's good just the way it is!" she said with conviction. "I thought about what you said last night, and I decided you might be right. I didn't know what to expect when I walked in there. But I sure never thought I'd decide that I didn't want it published if they were going to change it."

Andy could hardly believe this confident person was the same helpless Penny she'd seen curled up in the middle of a bed crying just yesterday. "So I went over to the journalism room to talk to them about the revision and they pulled my story and we started reading it together. Then I decided I liked the ending just like I wrote it, and I wanted them to print it that way.

"Well, she didn't agree with me right away, so I took the story and started to leave and that's when she said they'd reconsider the changes they wanted. But the important thing isn't whether they print my story. What really counts is that I *knew* I was right and if the

Journal didn't want to print it the way I wrote it, then I didn't want them to print it at all."

Andy stopped walking. "It sounds like it means a lot to you."

"Yeah, it does." Penny had stopped walking too and a look of awe was on her face. "I just didn't know how much until now. That's the first time in my life I've ever stood up for what I believed in. And once I finally did it, it didn't seem that bad." Penny smiled with satisfaction.

"But I will admit, I've spent so many years hearing everyone else tell me what I should do that it is kind of scary to think about deciding everything for myself. I mean, I could be wrong."

"Yeah, but you could be right too." Andy put her arm around Penny. "I'm so proud of you."

"I guess I'm proud of me too."

"Well, it looks like you might have discovered a real career for yourself," Jane said. "What are you planning to do from here?"

"I guess get serious about writing. Take some creative writing classes so that the next time I tell someone I think the story's good, I'll be more confident I'm right." The three of them laughed.

"I even know what my next story will be."

"Really?" Jane asked.

"Yep. It's going to be about this real perceptive girl from Texas who comes out East to this private school." Toby looked over at her suspiciously. "And when she gets there, she's able to figure things out pretty quick, because even though she hasn't spent a lot of time around people, she knows them pretty well. And sometimes she's the only one who can really see them like they are." Penny looked at Toby and both of them exchanged a knowing smile.

"Well, if you're going to get this career off to a good start you have to figure out a few things," Jane said. "Like have you decided if you're going to use a pen name or not?"

"No. I think I'll just use my own name. I sort of like it."

"Penny Vanderark," Andy said thoughtfully as they climbed the steps to Baker House.

"No," Penny said firmly. "Penelope Vanderark. It's the kind of name people can take seriously."

The four of them disappeared into Baker House and the sun reflected off the glass in the door as it glided shut behind them. No one looking at the quiet campus on that late spring afternoon would ever have believed the dreams that were being born, and the excitement that was exploding, behind those closed doors.

What should the girls of 407 do when a princess pays a visit to Canby Hall to see if she wants to go there, and falls in love — with a commoner? Read The Girls of Canby Hall #24, PRINCESS WHO?

APPLE® PAPERBACKS